"Now faith is the substance of things hoped for, the evidence of things unseen... Through faith we understand that the worlds were framed by the word of God, so that things which are seen were not made of things which do appear."

—Hebrews 11:1,3

Part I

CHAPTER ONE

Unfinished

The reason I left you in Crete was that you might straighten out what was left unfinished.
—Titus 1:5

Elisha Bookbinder rose early after a restless night, just as he had risen early after frequent sleepless nights of late. Half crawling, half falling out of his bed and wandering into the bathroom, he switched on the light and twisted the hot water tap. Outside the window, the sun had not yet risen. The night, Elisha realized with some annoyance, was unfinished. He could not help feeling that a great part of his world seemed unfinished in some ill-defined way he could not fully grasp, but which troubled him all the same. It didn't seem the sort of thought a rational mind ought to entertain.

Rubbing his eyes in an effort to bring them into focus, Elisha looked deeply into the dirty mirror hanging above the sink. There he saw a haggard and pale but otherwise familiar face. Nothing in that visage gave any hint of change, much less of a loosening grip on reality. If anything, he thought, the face staring at him looked not unfinished, but rather over-worn and past its prime. Search as he might, he detected not the least evidence of anything amiss that would explain the barely tangible yet undeniable sense of discontinuity that nagged at him.

Elisha cupped some hot water in his hands, lifted it to his face, and felt it warm his cheeks. He pulled a razor back and forth across his chin in a haphazard manner, quickly brushed his teeth, flicked the light switch off once again, and slipped back into bed, telling himself it would be for five minutes only, no more. When he had done so, a quite pleasant sense of peace washed over him, tempting him to yield unconditionally to the bed's familiar warmth and put off until tomorrow what would best be done this day. He closed his eyes for what he judged to be no more than a few seconds, but when he opened them once again, light had already begun to trickle in through his bedroom window and gently come to rest upon the room's furnishings.

Strange that the sun should rise so quickly, he thought.

His eyes followed the light around his bedroom, pausing as they fell upon familiar objects: his bathrobe hanging on the peg by the bathroom door, the quilt folded and hung over the stand beneath the Wyeth print, the leather-bound early edition of Dickens' *A Christmas Carol* that he'd been reading the night before. It was an annual habit, and with the holiday just around the corner, he had decided to renew it before ending an uneventful day. The book's badly worn spine needed mending, so he'd held it with the most loving care and turned each page ever so gently—a habit born of a love of old books and a lifetime of buying, selling, and handling them. He'd read most of Dickens' novels, beginning back in school when he'd had to study *A Tale of Two Cities* in English class and then do a report on it. Elisha wondered then, and still did, what made teachers think they could instill a love for books in kids by forcing them to do reports on them. Yet in Elisha's case, it had somehow worked. Or maybe it would be truer to say that it had failed to kill the love for books that formed an innate part of his nature.

He remembered some of the novels better than others. *The Mystery of Edwin Drood* had greatly intrigued him, as far as it went. But of course, it never quite got to where it was going, ending unfinished, like so many other great expectations Elisha had once had.

Of all Dickens' novels, *Bleak House*, hardly his most respected work, stuck most vividly in Elisha's mind, along with the refreshingly brief *Christmas Carol*. The *Carol* remained dear to Elisha ever since he'd played the role of Marley's ghost in a sixth -grade play. He could still recite his lines, or so he imagined, but he couldn't really be sure since he felt no inclination to try.

The recollection of his school days comforted him. The memories felt reassuringly finished, and it pleased him that he could remember such details from his own past. Yet that novella too was so frustratingly *unfinished*, though in an entirely different way than *The Mystery of Edwin Drood*. The author, he had always felt, came tantalizingly close to imparting something of real substance to his readers, only to mess everything up at the end and miss the point entirely. For all he could learn from Dickens, a reader might think Christmas was about nothing more than generosity and the domestic virtues. Humbug, to be sure. Was that what had troubled him so much that, once again, he had passed a restless night? Maybe he should sell the book, he thought. He couldn't go on much longer without a restful night's sleep, and if the *Carol* was even partially to blame, then maybe it would be for the best to part with it.

Yet surely, he told himself, there had to be more to this recent and inexplicable feeling of incompleteness than just the uninspiring climax to a story. The book was just one example, an unpleasant reminder of the sensation rather than the cause of it. Other reminders inhabited the corners of his life and hovered in the dimly lit crevasses of his consciousness. But then again, maybe not. Maybe they were only phantoms, by-products of his imagination, caused, likely as not, by an undigested blot of mustard. A part of him hoped not. The possibility that he might be losing his hold on reality irked him, and if such a thing were really happening, it would just drive him crazy, he told himself. Such an explanation for the haunted feeling he'd been living with could only end in total darkness. But another part of him reasoned that as long as his fears sprang forth from a muddled mind, then there was no real danger. In that case, the world would go on turning as it always had since the beginning of Creation, despite his ongoing sense of unease. If the problem lay in his own mind, he reassured himself, it may perhaps have a simple solution. Therapy or medication might set all to right. Maybe. But the more he thought about it, the less he felt sure what to think.

Again he wished that sleep would rescue him from his mental tumult, fearing that if he didn't soon settle himself, he'd begin the day with a headache that would linger till evening, or perhaps even longer. He tried concentrating on the familiar. On his robe, his quilt, anything but the book. Nothing, he told himself, could be more comforting than a warm, soft robe and an old-fashioned hand-stitched quilt. If he hoped to find peace of mind, these were the places to go hunting for it. He rose again from the bed and reached for the robe. The feel of the plush fabric felt good and familiar between his fingers. Sliding his arms into the sleeves, he noted with satisfaction the slightly frayed decorative stitching at each cuff. So *finished*, he mused. Every loose thread spoke of countless hours of wear and dozens of washings. He lifted the quilt from its stand and felt its weight in his arms. It comforted him to notice it had begun to fade unevenly, the result of bright afternoon sunlight that entered the room each day and advanced with relentless patience across the floor and partway up the wall where the quilt always hung. At that point, the sun dipped behind the eaves of his neighbor's large Victorian house, thus filling his bedroom with shadows. Such details seemed especially important now, and Elisha cherished each as a hopeful sign that the bland dreariness that had taken up lodging in his soul had not yet permeated every corner of his world. His quilt, at least, was multi-chromatic. Elisha knotted the cord of his robe, climbed back into bed for the third time in the past eight hours, and spread the quilt over top of him.

A new day had begun, but Elisha remained unwilling to participate. He knew already how he would feel, many hours from now, when midnight loomed and the dying day melted away. The clock on his night table would tell him that the day was done, but deep inside his soul, he would know differently. Some inexplicable sense would tell him, gently but persistently, that while the day might very well be gone, it had not been complete. For as long as he could remember, his days rarely were. Nor were the people he met. Nor was—and this was the most unsettling aspect of all—nor was his own history.

His past resembled a jigsaw puzzle with more than a few random pieces missing. Other memories seemed much larger and more prominent than they ought to be. He could remember parts of his childhood; the sixth-grade play and other details, and yet it all seemed so... What? Intangible was the only way he could describe it. Vague and unfinished. His memories seemed more like a collection of discrete events, rather than a stream flowing smoothly and inexorably from birth to adolescence. And yet, wasn't that the way of old memories—chock full of gaps and impossible contradictions?

"Do you remember that Christmas we all went to granddad's cabin and got caught in a blizzard?" one brother prompts another.

"No," says the other. "It was Thanksgiving, and it was at Uncle Bob's." And both brothers are dead certain that they remember it correctly.

So, Elisha wondered, why should it seem odd that he couldn't recall his first day of school (he couldn't) or learning to ride a bicycle (he didn't)? He couldn't say, but neither could he shake the disturbing notion that, somehow, those events had never happened. Yet his diploma hung on the wall of his small, musty bookshop, just behind the register, and he cycled to the bookstore every morning. Elisha didn't know quite what to make of it, but he knew enough to understand that he couldn't have graduated from a school he had not, at one time or another, attended for the first time. And that he couldn't get to work on a vehicle he had never learned to ride. So why couldn't he remember those events?

And it did not end with school days and cycling. It merely started there. Once he set his mind in motion, further examples occurred to him. In truth, there seemed no end to them. Neither was there any explanation, or none that Elisha's imagination could concoct. Lacking explanations, his mind instead brooded on dreams and foreboding, on books and robes and quilts.

Quilts and robes. They did feel good, for sure, good and heavy. The weight pressing down upon him as he lay beneath the quilt produced a reassuring sense of security—the way caterpillars must feel inside a cocoon. Or babies in the womb. Elisha recognized with detachment that his thoughts had grown disjointed and ungovernable, a sure sign that fatigue had caught up with him and that sleep, at last, had come to claim its inevitable victory. "An hour," he managed to tell himself through the fog that now enveloped his brain. "Just an hour before I'll need to leave for the shop." But what a blessed hour it would be. A holy hour of sacred sleep.

Formless noise coalesced in his mind, sounding as if it was rising up out of a deep well. Then, quickly, as if by command, the sounds organized themselves into the melody of a familiar song, and Elisha realized that it came from his clock radio, which he had set to wake himself at 6:30. Opening his eyes, he wondered that it seemed no brighter in the room than when he had fallen asleep. No matter, he felt surprisingly refreshed after so brief a nap and nearly managed a smile as he reached to turn off the alarm. He habitually tapped the snooze button every morning in order to claim another few minutes of rest before heading to the bathroom sink, but now he hardly felt the need. The digital dots and dashes on the clock face, he saw, formed the figures 6:38, and he snorted at the realization that the extra five minutes of rest he'd thought to forego had already come and gone. Somehow, he must have managed to sleep through eight minutes of rock music before his fatigued mind had registered the message and convinced his body to waken. Maybe he wasn't as well rested as he had first imagined.

In truth, Elisha was learning to distrust his imagination. It led him into places he preferred not to go: wild places where simple acts like riding his bicycle spawned endless questions. Now, it seemed, he could not even trust his imagination to know whether he was tired or well rested.

He shuffled into the bathroom once again and repeated the same morning ritual he had performed just a short while earlier, but in a somewhat brighter mood that continued to improve moment by moment. Yes, he *was* well rested, he decided. Wonderfully so. Inexplicably so. The door of the shower stall yielded to his push, and he stepped inside, feeling long overdue for a thorough, hot soak.

With a firm twist of the tap, a robust stream of water, shockingly cold for just a moment before quickly turning satisfyingly hot, sprayed his head and chest. Barely audible over the sound of the rushing water, the tune he had awoken to continued to play on the radio. It was an oldie, he knew. What was it called? Elisha was a bibliophile, but not a music lover *per se*. He enjoyed a wide variety of music in a casual way, but he couldn't name more than a handful of contemporary artists and was only marginally more familiar with the pop stars of his youth. His ability to name their tunes suffered as well. Without being conscious of it, he began humming along to the sound of the radio as he squeezed a dab of shampoo into his hand and worked it into his hair. The Beatles, he decided. *Across the Universe.*

Abruptly, the music faded and the melodious voice of the DJ replaced it, but over the shower, Elisha couldn't make out what he was saying. Identifying the song for all his listeners, he guessed. Within a few moments, another song began to play, one Elisha had never heard before. He finished rinsing the lather from his body, turned off the tap, and reached for his towel.

Back in his bedroom, Elisha methodically dressed. He looked into the depths of his closet to select a shirt and frowned. In the shadows, they all looked alike. It must be an overcast day, he thought. Usually, enough daylight found its way into even the closet's inner-most depths for him to manage without turning on the table lamp by his bedside. Well, this time he'd have to flip the switch, that's all. Otherwise, he mused, he was liable to leave the house wearing who knows what. Maybe that horrid paisley monstrosity he'd received as a gift from his well-intentioned mother the previous Christmas.

He turned on the lamp and its one-hundred-watt bulb glowed to life. But the light chilled him. In a flash, Elisha became acutely conscious of remembering the lamp for the first time. Or rather, he remembered what he was fairly certain had never before been. The lamp, in fact, had never existed until he remembered it. It sat atop the table covered with a dusty veneer that indicated a long his-tory, but Elisha knew—he *knew*!—that it had not existed until just moments before. There had, in fact, been no need for it to exist. Natural sunlight made it unnecessary. Except on this particular dark day. And now, just as a need for it arose, it had appeared in his unfinished world, one more piece of a still far-from-finished puzzle that had inexplicably fallen into place at just the necessary moment. And along with it, Elisha realized, had appeared a ready-made mem-ory doing its best to convince him that the lamp had been there all along and that he had seen it on countless mornings before this one. But Elisha wasn't fooled. Real memories have a distinct quality that demands they be trusted, but which this memory lacked. This memory, he knew at once, was an illusion, a fraud. It was a memory of something that never was, planted into his mind in order to make him believe it had always been. But how, and why?

Elisha's head spun, and he felt a sudden, urgent need to be somewhere else, as if his own bedroom had been bewitched and become a dangerous and alien place. All concerns over matching socks fled him, and he carelessly threw on the first pair of pants and the first shirt he found in his closet and dresser drawers, then hurried downstairs into the kitchen, half afraid of what he might find there. To his relief, he saw no lamps that had never existed. In fact, all seemed mundanely familiar, and real. Reassured, and embarrassed at what he began to think had been a moment of childish panic, akin to a young boy's absolute certainty that a monster lived in his closet and was about to pounce, Elisha forced himself to take a deep breath and slowly counted to ten. And then, just to be on the safe side, to twenty. Feeling better, he dropped a slice of bread into the toaster (which he felt confident had been there the night before) and went looking into the refrigerator for some jam, which was nowhere to be found. The beginnings of a new wave of panic welled up inside him until he recalled quite clearly that he had finished the jar the day before and thrown it in the trash.

Or was he just imagining that too? Impulsively, he turned the trash can over and dumped its contents onto the kitchen floor. As he did so, an empty jar of orange marmalade hit the linoleum and then rolled under a cabinet. So yes, he *had* finished it the day before. He took another, even deeper breath, feeling some relief that in this one small matter, at least, his memories matched his perceptions. But rather than risk another turn of fortune, he left the dry toast on the counter, untouched, and headed for the door.

He stepped outside and braced himself for yet another workday, hoping the distraction would do him some good. A little bit of dull routine might be just what he needed. If anything, the sky was even darker than before, but he forced himself not to think about it as he straddled the seat of his bicycle.

"Getting kind of a late start today, aren't you, Elisha?" called out Mrs. Chancellor, his kind-hearted next-door neighbor.

"Huh, what's that?" answered the self-conscious bookseller.

"Why, it's past dinnertime. Just where to do think you're off to?"

And with that, it all became clear. It hadn't taken eight minutes for Elisha to awaken after his alarm had gone off—it had taken twelve hours and eight minutes. Now, the day was drawing to a close, not so much unfinished as never even haven gotten started.

Without a word, Elisha trudged back inside, reluctantly headed back upstairs, flopped down on the bed from which he had so recently risen, and laid there for the rest of the evening and through a long, sleepless night.

CHAPTER TWO

Merely Players

For the revelation awaits an appointed time;
it speaks of the end
and will not prove false.
—Habakkuk 2:3

O f course, all was not really clear. Not by a long shot. All that Elisha's alarm clock mishap really explained was why he'd felt so rested upon rising. And that only explained why he wasn't ready to sleep again until just about 6:30 the following morning, when his alarm again went off. But it didn't explain why his life seemed so unfinished or the bedside table lamp that had stood next to his bed for ages—but only since last evening. Elisha got to his feet more quickly this time, though hardly with alacrity and certainly not feeling the least refreshed. He showered and dressed. The bright morning sun made the lamp unnecessary, but he instinctively knew that needed or not, now that it had appeared it would remain there forever unless he personally removed it.

Downstairs, he breakfasted on two slices of fresh, warm toast. Remembering the marmalade jar lying out of sight underneath the hutch, he fetched it and returned it to the trashcan. Then he once again exited through the front door. This time, however, Mrs.

Chancellor greeted him with a warm, "Good morning, Elisha. Have a wonderful day at the shop."

The crisp morning air bit at his nose and cheeks, helping chase the sluggishness from his head as he pedaled the seven miles to the edge of town, to the ramshackle—no, rustic, he corrected himself—old grist mill that he'd given a second life when he'd acquired it for next-to-nothing and converted it into an emporium for the buying and selling of used and rare books. A really first-rate used bookshop has a certain not-unpleasant smell of age, and Elisha's shop reeked of it. Nestled in a tree-lined hollow less than a mile from a busy intersection, it provided customers with a convenient location not far from the local bank, post office, and convenience store, and offered Elisha a secluded retreat from the same. The book dealer felt no shame or hesitation in calling himself old-fashioned. His quaint ways and simple outlook endeared him to his patrons. Elisha's books, his business, and his demeanor were all of a piece, holdovers from a happier time when books were printed on paper and deals were sealed with a handshake and sellers really cared about satisfying their customers. Elisha certainly did. He loved his chosen trade and genuinely enjoyed working at it.

His outlook brightened as he unlocked the old wooden door and swung it open. According to his daily custom, he paused long enough to select three pieces of split hickory wood from the stack by the door, then headed inside and carried them to the pot-bellied stove that was the shop's first line of defense against the cold. With less than a week to go until Christmas and a biting chill in the air, a good twenty minutes would pass before the inside temperature rose enough to permit him to comfortably remove his plaid overcoat. He didn't mind. When January arrived, he knew, he'd need to turn on the forced-air heater, but he preferred the ambiance created by the less efficient stove. There is a sort of warmth that doesn't register on a thermometer, which only a wood stove can provide.

His shop had a simple, comfortable, and crudely finished feel to it, so that even though wintry drafts penetrated seams in the roughly finished plank walls on windy days, and the unbearable summer heat necessitated that he close shop each August and take an unwanted vacation, he avoided renovating the shop by installing insulation or central air.

Elisha judged that the main floor would be warm well before ten o'clock, when he expected a very special customer to arrive. He'd telephoned the week before, pricking Elisha's interest with an offer to bring in an 1880 leather-bound edition of *The Works of Shakespeare*, published by Ginn & Company and in very fine condition, according to the owner. Elisha had hastened to assure the caller of his interest and made an appointment to see the volume for himself. In fact, he was already certain he would buy it regardless of the price, but it would be foolish to say so. Elisha hoped his voice had not betrayed his eagerness to hold the edition in his own hands, thereby inadvertently tipping off the seller to ask top dollar.

In retrospect, it had probably been a mistake to schedule the appointment so early in the morning. It betrayed a childish excitement that the seller could too easily exploit, but Elisha hadn't been able to help himself. Shakespeare had that effect on him. His plays, especially his histories, seemed so satisfyingly finished. They reassured as much as enthralled Elisha. Five tidy acts at a time, the Bard reconstructed a glorious past, pulled back the curtain on deeds both foul and fair, unveiled villains and introduced conflict, and then deftly resolved the same in unambiguous climaxes that left no loose threads to trouble a reader's mind or keep him awake at night. The world in which Shakespeare's characters walked featured brilliant whites and pitch blackness, and even the shades of gray were sharply delineated—carefully crafted to produce in the reader's mind the exact freely-arrived-at response the author had prepared them for in advance. Such great stories, so deftly constructed, deserved to be read and reread from a truly rare and fine edition, and Elisha intended to have it.

By 10:04, he could barely stand the wait and had to remind himself that calling to ask about the delay would be unwise. Much better to simply find a way to pass the time until the book and its owner arrived. Elisha excelled at passing time, having had frequent occasion to hone the skill. Shuffling across the sales floor, he headed behind the counter to a shelf hidden from the view of customers, which held several volumes he had just recently purchased at auction and had not yet had a chance to inventory and place throughout the shop. He renewed a game he often played with himself—pick the very first book he came to among the new purchases and read it regardless of what the title, author, or subject might be. Reaching toward the shelf, he retrieved a volume at random and looked expectantly at the spine: *The Mystery of Edwin Drood.* He sighed. No, he thought, he couldn't bring himself to begin, knowing that it would never end. He selected the adjacent volume instead, which strictly speaking was against the rules of his game, but he reasoned that since he had made the rules himself he was entitled to change them as needed. He read the title on the second book: *Bleak House.* Fate, it seemed, ordained that Dickens would be his companion this day, no matter how many rules Elisha broke. Well, it was worth another read, he supposed. He took a seat in the wooden high-backed rocking chair he kept by the stove and opened it to the first page:

> Fog everywhere. Fog up the river, where it flows among green aits and meadows; fog down the river, where it rolls defiled among the tiers of shipping and the waterside pollutions of a great (and dirty) city. Fog on the Essex marshes, fog on the Kentish heights. Fog creeping into the cabooses of collier-brigs; fog lying out on

the yards and hovering in the rigging of great ships; fog drooping on the gunwales of barges and small boats. Fog in the eyes and throats of ancient Greenwich pensioners, wheezing by the firesides of their wards; fog in the stem and bowl of the afternoon pipe of the wrathful skipper, down in his close cabin; fog cruelly pinching the toes and fingers of his shivering little 'prentice boy on deck...

Much like this morning, Elisha thought. Exactly like this morning, in fact. It was almost as if the Good Lord had been reading *Bleak House* himself when deciding what sort of day this should be and had used Dickens as his inspiration. Elisha chuckled to himself at the absurdity of the thought and felt pleased that he was able to do so. He must be starting to relax if he could find humor in a fog. What other things might God have in store for him on this day if the Almighty had indeed been enjoying Dickens and taking his cues from *Bleak House*, he mused? He continued reading. The increasing warmth from the wood fire and the unhurried pace of the novel combined with his lack of sleep and growing sense of relaxation to make Elisha drowsy. He read on but without heeding the words or noticing the passage of time, until...

At a quarter till eleven, the shop door swung open to reveal a man carrying a large volume tucked under his arm. "Mr. Bookbinder?" he asked. Elisha nodded. "Drew Unwin. Sorry I'm late. It's a deuce of a fog out there. Couldn't see more than a few yards in front of me. Took me forever to get here. Then I drove right by your place without realizing it. Had to come back around for another go."

"Yes," Elisha allowed, "fog everywhere."

"And damp as the dickens. Feels nice in here though. Lovely shop. Lots of character. I feel like I've stepped into the pages of an old novel."

Elisha felt pleased by the comparison. "Thank you." He pointed at the book Unwin held tightly against his overcoat. "Is that the volume we talked about?"

"It is. May I show it to you?"

"Very well," Elisha answered, trying not to sound as eager as he felt.

Mr. Unwin held *The Works of Shakespeare* in both hands and slowly rotated it before Elisha's eyes so he could see it from every angle. "Good solid binding with no cracking, and not a trace of foxing. You won't find a copy in better condition anywhere." He set it on the counter and proudly opened the cover. "Beautiful endpapers," he noted, "and just take a look at the typography. The physical quality of this edition appeals to the eye no less than the Bard's words delight the ear. You're an admirer of Shakespeare I presume?"

This time Elisha didn't trust himself to say anything so he merely nodded. It hardly mattered as Unwin rambled on without listening for a response. "My favorite is *As You Like It*." He flipped gingerly through the pages. "Let's see, where is that bit I like? Ahh here it is!" He recited the lines:

> All the world's a stage,
> And all the men and women merely players:
> They have their exits and their entrances;
> And one man in his time plays many parts,
> His acts being seven ages. At first the infant,
> Mewling and puking in the nurse's arms.
> And then the whining school-boy, with his satchel
> And shining morning face, creeping like snail
> Unwillingly to school. And then the lover,

Sighing like furnace, with a woeful ballad
Made to his mistress' eyebrow. Then a soldier,
Full of strange oaths and bearded like the pard,
Jealous in honour, sudden and quick in quarrel,
Seeking the bubble reputation
Even in the cannon's mouth. And then the justice,
In fair round belly with good capon lined,
With eyes severe and beard of formal cut,
Full of wise saws and modern instances;
And so he plays his part. The sixth age shifts
Into the lean and slipper'd pantaloon,
With spectacles on nose and pouch on side,
His youthful hose, well saved, a world too wide
For his shrunk shank; and his big manly voice,
Turning again toward childish treble, pipes
And whistles in his sound. Last scene of all,
That ends this strange eventful history,
Is second childishness and mere oblivion,
Sans teeth, sans eyes, sans taste, sans everything.

Elisha hadn't been listening since the second line of the soliloquy. Upon hearing the words, "All the men and women merely players" a tingle had shot up his spine and now his palms were moist with sweat. The room seemed unseasonably warm and he wondered momentarily whether he had thrown too much wood into the old stove. What a strange effect Jaques' words imparted upon his long-troubled mind! Answers to questions that had never yet occurred to him shot fully wrought through his soul. The most improbable possibilities sprang spontaneously into his consciousness, some dispersing almost as quickly as they had formed, while others—the least likely of all—lingered and coalesced and even grew. A vision of things undreamt-of gradually formed in his head, as if a curtain slowly but deliberately drew back, revealing things previously unseen and even unsuspected. And yet alongside these fantastical and unbidden thoughts grew an unconquerable certainty that strange and unwelcome as they might be, they could not be refuted.

All of the unlikely plot twists in the pulp science fiction pot-boilers crowding Elisha's rustic bookstore couldn't compare to the probabilities now taking shape inside his brain. None of the ramblings of the great thinkers whose lifework filled the shelves in the philosophy alcove had anticipated the shocking worldview that Elisha irreversibly converted to in that moment when the simple phrase "All the men and women merely players" forever transformed him.

Had Shakespeare known? Had his play been a warning in disguise, intended to alert readers and audiences to its awful significance? No, Elisha understood in an instant. Jaques' soliloquy was undoubtedly a coincidence, a mere fortuitous choice of words meant to convey something else entirely. But nonetheless his words embodied truth—a truth far deeper and wider than the Bard himself imagined, the most critical, life-changing truth that ever could be!

Elisha needed to be alone with his thoughts, to ponder them, weigh them, and then... what? What exactly could one do, *should* one do, in response to revelations such as these? All interest in the complete works of Shakespeare, certainly, had vanished entirely, save for those seven extraordinary words. Elisha needed time to gather his rampaging thoughts.

"Excuse me, Mr. Unwin," he said. "I just remembered a previous appointment... Silly of me to forget it... Most urgent. I need to see to it right away... Unavoidable, I assure you. May we conclude this business some other time? So sorry... Let me show you to the door."

Under other circumstances, Elisha's abrupt conclusion to the visit would have offended Unwin, but he could see that something had agitated his host and assumed he must have said something to deeply offend the shop's owner. A sense of guilt rather than resentment welled up within him, and embarrassed by the thought of what his host must think of him for whatever *faux pas* he had inadvertently committed, he too suddenly succumbed to an immediate and overwhelming desire to remove himself from the situation. Muttering an apologetic "So sorry," and slipping a business card into Elisha's hand, he hastened toward the door and into his car even faster than Elisha could shoo him on, pulling the door shut behind him on his way out.

Elisha peeped out the corner window until he saw Unwin's BMW turn from the gravel lot onto the macadam road and head back toward town, then he flipped the sign in his window over so that instead of reading "Open," it informed patrons, "Sorry, We're Closed." He pulled down the shades so that persistent or skeptical visitors would not peer in and see him sitting alone among his books and knock on the door hoping to persuade him to reopen.

Having thus safeguarded himself against unwelcome intruders, he next cut a deliberate path to the washroom. He turned on the tap and leaned over the sink while he splashed the refreshing, clear water onto his face. He doused himself repeatedly until his face and forehead had cooled, then he rose, looked vacantly at his reflection in the mirror, and turned to leave without bothering to dry himself.

All the while his mind churned. He felt excessively self-conscious. The sensation was similar, he imagined, to what a microbe might feel if it could know and understand that its every movement was being examined under a microscope. Yet that wasn't quite right. There was even more to it. He felt like a marionette connected by invisible strings to a master manipulator. He disliked the sensation.

Elisha deliberately bit his lip, felt funny about having done so, and wished he hadn't. Where were these odd thoughts coming from? He was sure he knew. "Get a grip on yourself, old boy," he said out loud, "'Tis not yet time for your second childishness." Strangely, conversing with himself in an empty shop seemed more natural than anything else he'd done since receiving his revelation. And that, he reasoned, was because if his revelation was true, he wasn't really alone at all, never had been, and never could be.

CHAPTER THREE

Déjà vu in Reverse

Listen, I tell you a mystery....
—1 Corinthians 15:51a

Elisha left the shop, mounted his cycle, and pedaled back out of the hollow, up the same slope he had descended barely an hour earlier. His mind raced with questions to the answer that Shakespeare had so starkly revealed to him. The answer demanded a response, but of what kind? And was the choice even up to him? Did he have any choice at all, or were his actions in this life all predetermined? But if that were true, then maybe even his questions were predetermined. Not that it really mattered—they came to him regardless, and disturbed him all the same. He knew his priorities would never again be the same, then wondered in a detached sort of way whether he'd ever return to his shop or sell another book, and felt a palpable sense of dismay when he realized that, ultimately, it probably didn't matter.

Who was doing all this to him? Or would it be more correct to ask, who was doing this *with* him? And, after all, he lamented, why me? But that thought only led inevitably to another dawning realization even more disturbing than the first. It wasn't just him after all, was it? It couldn't be. That wouldn't make any sense. No, he told himself, it couldn't be that way. It wasn't him; it was *everyone*! And not even just every*one*, but every*thing*, and every *place*. All the world really *was* a stage, wasn't it? And all the men and women he had ever known—his kindergarten teacher, his mailman, the unsuspecting Mr. Unwin—all really *were* merely players.

Did any of them know? Of course not, he reasoned. No one suspected the truth. Except him. What might they do if confronted with it? Would it drive them mad, as Elisha feared it was already driving him? How might they deal with it? How *could* they deal with it, or was that too determined in advance? Maybe they simply didn't have the capacity to comprehend the nature of this new reality Elisha had stumbled onto. That could be, he decided. Maybe comprehension simply ran contrary to the physical laws of this new universe he'd discovered. But no. It couldn't be after all. He had figured it out. That meant others could too. They'd just have to be convinced. Shown the evidence. He sighed again. What evidence? There wasn't any, really. Not of the kind that would be likely to persuade ordinary people. People with careers to pursue and children to raise and problems of their own to solve. If he tried to tell them of his discovery, they'd only laugh at him. And he'd have no cause to blame them. He'd have done the same if yesterday some well-intentioned soul intruded upon his complaisant existence with the outlandish and unwelcome news that his very existence was more myth than matter, more player than person.

But again, his next conscious thought directly contradicted its antecedent. No. Evidence existed after all. One just needed to learn how to recognize it, because it took the strangest and most unexpected shapes, like that of a table lamp. Evidence solid and persuasive enough to explain his own irreversible conviction that his discovery was true hid in plain sight, in everyday events and unremarkable objects. It was not the kind of evidence you could measure or weigh or hold in your hand or affix a label to, but that didn't make it any less real. This sort of evidence wouldn't convince people of a certain predisposition, but they couldn't blame the evidence for that, only their own myopia. But they *would* blame the evidence nonetheless. And they would laugh at him, many of them, and tell him he had to do better if he expected them to put any stock in his wild ideas. They'd tell him his evidence simply wouldn't do, even though it had been sufficient to allow him to discern the truth, and if he could put all the pieces together, then they were without excuse, whatever they might say. This chain of thought made him dizzy, but he needed to think it through nevertheless.

Maybe he could help them understand. He could explain it all to them. In fact, he had a responsibility to explain it. The truth he had discovered changed everything. *Everything.* And it wouldn't do to keep it bottled up. If not simply to avoid bursting like an overripe melon, then for the sake of dispelling the ignorance of billions of his neighbors and helping them to make a necessary shift in priorities, he needed to reveal the secret he had so unintentionally stumbled upon.

But where to start, and who to tell first? He instinctively felt that calling the newspapers would be a grievous mistake. Not yet anyway. They'd just hang up on him, or worst yet, expose him to such ridicule that no one would give him a second chance. That would be as far as his revelation would go. He needed to find a better way. First he'd feel out a close friend. If he couldn't convince a friend, he'd have scant chance of winning any converts among the press. But therein lay the next problem. He simply didn't *have* any close friends. Well, all right then, he decided, a close acquaintance would have to do. He had several of those. He'd broach the subject carefully, building slowly and logically up to the truth. He'd do it gently, like a parent waking a sleepwalking child and assuring him that all he'd been chasing after had only been a dream, although in this case there really was no chance of waking up. There could only be the emerging understanding that the dream would go on and on forever. But so be it. If he could convince an acquaintance or two, then he'd gain the confidence he'd need in order to go to the papers, and at the same time, he'd gain experience in presenting a convincing case.

He realized to his satisfaction that his thoughts had been gradually gaining cohesion. They no longer assaulted him in a furious barrage; he'd regained his command of them. His imagination once again obeyed orders from his reason. He had a plan. Things had turned a corner, he told himself. He still couldn't say whether this was all predetermined, but until he could say for sure that it was, he'd act on the assumption that he remained lord over his own destiny.

Elisha pedaled to his front stoop and dismounted. He removed his helmet and hung it by the strap over one handlebar. It occurred to him that until just that moment, he had no memory of buying the helmet or of ever wearing one when he rode. But whereas just hours before such a realization would have filled him with puzzlement and concern for his mental well-being, now he smiled knowingly to himself. "Evidence," he said out load.

"What's that you said, dear?" The voice belonged to Mrs. Chancellor.

Elisha glanced up at her and opened his mouth as if to reply, but hesitated.

"Are you okay, Elisha?" she asked. "You only left for the shop a short while ago. Are you feeling under the weather?" She felt slightly embarrassed over taking such an obvious interest in the younger man's business. "I don't mean to pry now, dear. You know that isn't my way, but you just haven't been yourself lately, and well, I do get concerned for you. I hope you're not offended."

Elisha couldn't help feeling warmed by her concern. "Not at all, Mrs. Chancellor. You needn't worry. I'm feeling well." Strictly speaking, that was true. Elisha knew there was plenty more to be said, but not how to broach the subject.

His neighbor took note of his awkward silence and correctly sensed he needed some encouragement to speak his mind. "I tell you what, dear," she offered. "Why don't you come inside? I just made some cookies, and I'd like you to try one and tell me if you think I added too much sugar."

Elisha smiled. He thought it odd that each of them could so easily understand the other even though neither found it easy to say what they really meant. But he was grateful that it was so and accepted both the cookie and the selfless concern that lay behind the offer.

They entered the house, and Elisha realized he'd never before been inside his neighbor's home. He'd said "Good day" to Mrs. Chancellor nearly every morning on his way out his own door, and then "Good evening" upon his return, but their relationship had never amounted to anything more. He couldn't even remember ever seeing her anywhere around town, only right there in her own front yard, doing some weeding in the garden, or watering the grass, or fetching mail from the box. He shared his thoughts with her.

"Well, now," she said thoughtfully, "I suppose that's right. I don't get out and about as much as I should, it's true, but I just don't feel motivated, by and large. I'm not one of those people who's always on the go. I enjoy keeping to myself, and if I go out, it's just to take in the sights and the fresh air I can enjoy from my own front stoop. I guess that sounds awfully dull to a man as active as you, hmm?"

"No, not really," Elisha assured her. "It's not all that different with me. I'm not nearly as active as you imagine. Yes, I hop on my bicycle every morning, but just long enough to ride to the shop. Once there, I spend most of my days reading. Now and then a customer or two stops by, and when they do, I ask whether they're looking for anything special. If they are, I help them find it. Otherwise I tell them they're free to browse. If they find something, I take their money. If not, I wish them a good day. Either way I'm back into my books again as soon as the door swings shut behind them. I like things that way. So I can understand why you enjoy keeping to yourself and tinkering in your front yard. I imagine you find it relaxing."

"Yes, you do understand. Very relaxing. You might say it's all I was made for."

And in a flash, it occurred to Elisha that she was almost certainly right. Tinkering was literally all she was made for. That and this very conversation. He briefly wondered whether he should feel sorry for her, but decided against it. If she was doing what she was made for, that had to be a good thing, didn't it? He wasn't quite sure. But her comment brought him back to the reason he had wanted to talk with her in the first place and provided him with a good place to start.

"Mrs. Chancellor, I've had a lot on my mind lately, and I think you may be just the person to help me sort it all out."

Mrs. Chancellor seemed genuinely surprised. "Oh! However can I be of help?"

Elisha squirmed. Without intending to, she had hit upon the very question Elisha felt least prepared to answer. "Well, let me start at the beginning" he said, hoping to buy some time to think of something more to the point. For a moment, he hoped that maybe she'd say something to help him get started, but when he saw her simply looking on with great interest and saintly patience, he began with a question. "Mrs. Chancellor, have you ever been in this room before?"

He knew it was a dangerous tactic. She could very well laugh at him, thinking it to be some sort of jest, and then take nothing else he had to say the least bit seriously. And indeed her reaction led him to fear that's exactly what she did think. "Why, of course I have. I live here. I've spent most of my life in this house, and a good deal of that time sitting here in the kitchen baking cookies and pies. This room is my universe."

Elisha had known this wouldn't be easy, so her answer failed to dissuade him from continuing. "Mrs. Chancellor, humor me. I want you to really concentrate. I know it seems to you right now that you've always lived in this house and enjoyed baking your cookies right here in your kitchen, but do think hard. Before you invited me in to have a cookie, would you have been able to describe this room to me?"

Mrs. Chancellor played along. Her face clearly revealed that she thought this a silly game of some sort, but kind-heartedness came easily to her and she genuinely wanted to be of comfort to her distressed neighbor, so she concentrated on his question just as he had requested.

As he watched from across the kitchen table, Elisha saw the corners of her lips curl upward as an indulgent smile momentarily played across her face, then as quickly it vanished, to be replaced by an emotionless stare, then a slight frown, and finally a look of puzzlement.

"You can't remember, can you?" Elisha prompted.

"Well, now, it's odd but don't you know, it does seem somehow that there's a strangeness about this room. And yet at the same time, I feel so comfortable and familiar here. I don't know exactly how to describe it. Maybe like déjà vu in reverse. Instead of seeing something for the first time and thinking it looks familiar, I feel like I'm seeing familiar things for the first time."

"Yes, that's a good way of putting it. That's exactly what it's like."

"You feel it too?"

"Yes. I've been feeling it for weeks."

"Well," Mrs. Chancellor abruptly concluded, "I wouldn't worry about it. A little episode of déjà vu never caused anyone any harm."

"But it's not déjà vu, Mrs. Chancellor. You said so yourself. It's only more or less like déjà vu, but in reverse." Elisha could tell that his rather risky way of getting round to the subject had paid off. Mrs. Chancellor's interest had been piqued. But so too had her anxiety. The frown had returned to her face, and it looked as if it might be settling in for a prolonged stay.

"Think, Mrs. Chancellor. That toaster over there. Where did you buy that?"

"Well," she intoned after a moment's hesitation, "nowhere, really. I think I've just always had it. I mean, it must be a hand-me-down. From my mother probably."

"Do you remember your mother?"

By now the kindly woman looked as if she seriously regretted inviting Elisha into her home.

"My m-mother?"

"Yes," Elisha shot back. "Quickly, describe her to me."

"It's hard. It's been so long and well... Well, yes, just a moment. It's coming back to me. She was short. Quite short, in fact. Her name was... Madeline, but she went by Maddie. Blue eyes, I think... Yes, definitely blue. And eyeglasses. That's right. I remember. She needed them for distances, but when she was reading, she'd prop them up on top of her head. And then she'd forget they were up there, and she'd spend forever trying to find where she'd put them. When I came home from school, she'd tell me 'I did it again!' and we'd both have a good laugh over it."

Elisha continued pressing. "But you didn't remember that at first, did you? When I first asked you about your mother, you drew a blank, didn't you? I could see it by your expression. No one should have trouble remembering her own mother, but you didn't, did you? Not until we began talking about her and there was a need for you to remember. Then the memories appeared, ready-made, and you were able to share them with me."

Maddie's daughter said nothing, a clear indication that Elisha had guessed correctly. "Oh dear." She sniffled. "It's not fair. I'm not a well-to-do person. My memories are all that I've ever had to cling to, and now age and a feeble mind are taking those from me too. What'll I do when they are gone for good?"

Elisha felt terrible that he had upset her so, but there was more to it than the typical effects of advancing age, of course. Would the truth reassure her or upset her even more? Elisha couldn't begin to guess. The truth had certainly thrown him for a loop, but it might actually be a relief to someone who feared she was suffering from the early stages of dementia.

"Take heart, Mrs. Chancellor. It's not that you've lost any memories, or that you're in any danger of such a thing. Just the opposite. It's not that you forgot your mother. It's that up until just a moment ago, she never existed."

CHAPTER FOUR

Unnecessary Parts

*I have become [a] servant by the commission God gave
me to present to you the word of God in its fullness—
the mystery that has been kept hidden for ages and
generations, but is now disclosed to the saints.*
—*Colossians 1:25–26*

Mrs. Chancellor had been listening sympathetically to Elisha up to that point, and even found much of what he had to say curiously interesting, but she could make nothing of his latest bombshell. "Oh now, Elisha, that's just silly. Of course she existed. She's gone now, of course. She died years ago. That's why I had to think a bit before I could remember her face. But it's clear to me now. I was her only child. She raised me on her own after Daddy died, at least until I got my own place. Even then I phoned her every day for years and years, right up to the time when—well, when she started having trouble and then she couldn't remember who I was and my calls only agitated her so I had to stop. But I remember her. And, well, after all, everybody has a mother. You simply can't get around it."

"I know, Mrs. Chancellor, I know. That's what I always thought too. And I know this is hard to believe. But I'm convinced it's true.

It's the same with me. There are things in my past that are just miss-ing, like your mother was until just now."

"Missing?"

"Yes. For example, you see me get on my bicycle every morning and ride to my bookshop, right?"

"Yes, but what of it?"

"Do you know that I never learned to ride a bike?"

"Sure you did. You ride all the time. Elisha, you're confusing me."

"I'm sorry. Let me try to be clearer. Yes, I know how to ride now, but I never learned back then. I have no memory of such a thing."

"Well then you forgot. Everyone forgets things. Like I did with my mother just now."

Elisha shook his head. He wasn't getting anywhere, and he sensed Mrs. Chancellor's frustration growing. She might send him away at any moment and refuse to talk about it anymore. He began speaking more quickly in order to make it harder for her to interrupt. "I didn't forget. I'm sure of it. It never happened. There's no need for it to have happened. It's not a part of my story, you see? So it's been left out. That's how it works—a good story, I mean. You decide what's important for your reader to know and then you tell him, but you leave the unnecessary parts out. They'd just sidetrack the story."

Mrs. Chancellor didn't follow the logic and couldn't think of anything to say, but in order to keep the conversation moving on toward a conclusion as promptly as possible, she nodded her head as if in agreement.

"But we can change that. I'll show you. Ask me to tell you all about how I learned to ride a bike."

"But you just said you never did."

"I didn't! Not yet. But go ahead and ask me."

Elisha knew right then that he had picked the right person to share his discovery with. Anyone else would surely have shown him the door and locked it behind him, but Mrs. Chancellor played along, if only because she couldn't think of anything else to do. "Well, okay, Elisha. How then? Tell me how you learned to ride a bike."

"Right now?" That caught her off guard and made her wonder if she'd fallen into some sort of a cleverly set trap. Elisha could see the hesitation in her eyes, so he nodded his head to indicate what answer he wanted her to give.

"Yes, right now," she responded on cue.

Elisha screwed his eyes shut tight and a look of intense concentration came across his face. Then, in just a few moments, he broke into a smile that stretched from ear to ear. He began giggling, which Mrs. Chancellor interpreted as a bad sign, until he shouted, "It worked! I remember! Or, maybe that's not the right word. I just know now. I know how it happened."

"How you learned to ride a bicycle, you mean?"

"Exactly! Let me tell you. I was at the school playground. That's where my brother used to take me to practice. He'd ride there with me holding on behind him, then he'd climb off and run alongside me while I tried to pedal and steer and stay upright. I remember him saying that my birthday was getting close, and if I could learn to ride in time, maybe Mom and Dad would surprise me with my own bike. But only if I could show them I was able to ride it. And it worked. I'd been pretty half-hearted in my efforts to learn up until then, but the thought of getting my own brand-new bike made me try that much harder, and by the end of that afternoon, I could ride back home with my big brother holding on behind *me. That's* how it happened!"

Mrs. Chancellor didn't understand at all, but it sounded to her as if her neighbor had reached some sort of epiphany and that the conversation must be drawing to an end. "Well, that's wonderful, really. Such a nice story. I'm so glad you remembered it."

"But you still don't understand." Mrs. Chancellor knew that much already. "I haven't really remembered. That memory wasn't there before you asked me. It's new. It's just been put into my head."

"Isn't that interesting?" Mrs. Chancellor's efforts to remain politely cheerful grew ever more difficult and less convincing. But Elisha had brought her to the brink of the truth and was ready to put the final piece of the puzzle into place.

"Listen, Mrs. Chancellor. You've read novels, right?"

Another hesitant nod.

"Did you ever wonder what it would be like to be one of the characters in a novel?" Nodding seemed to be working well, Mrs. Chancellor noted, so she made a decision to answer all further questions that way.

"Mrs. Chancellor, you don't need to wonder what it would be like. You already know. You see, you and me and everyone you've ever met or heard about aren't real. We're all just characters in a story. Figments of the Author's imagination, living lives that he's writing for us. Or maybe the Author is a woman. I haven't figured that part out yet."

Even a nod seemed recklessly encouraging at this point, so Mrs. Chancellor remained both speechless and motionless.

"That's why I couldn't remember learning to ride my bicycle," Elisha continued without pause. "It simply wasn't a part of the story. It had never needed to be told. The Author, as best as I can tell, began his story after I'd already become an adult. So much of my childhood got left out. He never wrote it in. You see? It makes sense, doesn't it? I can't be expected to remember something he never wrote into my childhood. But we forced his hand, see? When I told you to ask me how I learned to ride my bike, it forced me to answer and in order for me to give you an answer, the Author needed to create one for me. He had to add it to the story. Or *she* did, maybe."

Mrs. Chancellor had an idea. Maybe if she glanced at her watch, Elisha would think that she was late for some appointment and would graciously end their conversation. But he failed to take notice.

"And it's why you didn't remember what your own kitchen looked like. Up until now, I never talked to you in here—only in your front yard. So the story never needed a kitchen before this. It was only just written into our lives a few minutes ago. And it's the same with your mother. She's not a part of the story either, so the Author never wrote her into existence until I asked you to think of her. Then he had to create a memory for you so you could tell me about her. We're all just players, you see? Like Shakespeare said."

This last bit went completely over Mrs. Chancellor's head, but then again, so had nearly everything else Elisha had spoken since entering the house. Silence followed Elisha's outburst while each waited for the other to add something to what had already been said. Mrs. Chancellor had no intention of making the attempt, and Elisha eventually relented. He'd done his best. It was time to retreat, take stock, and weigh his options.

"Well, anyway, I thought you ought to know. I'm sorry if I've upset you. I'll see my own way out." And he did. Shuffling absent-mindedly through the front door, he returned to his own familiar home and climbed the stairs to his bedroom. His eyes scanned the familiar surroundings searching for any changes. There seemed to be none, yet even so, everything felt different. Nothing his eyes took in felt real. But then the meaning of the very word "real" had changed since he'd left home earlier this same morning. If he was only a manifestation of someone's imagination, did that make him any less real? He pinched himself, feeling foolish as he did so. He sure felt real. But then again, how was a character in a story supposed to feel? For that matter, what did being a real, living, actual person feel like? If he was right (and he knew he was), then he had never been a real person and had therefore never felt the sort of feelings a real person might feel.

So how could he tell the difference? He heard himself whimpering softly to himself, felt embarrassed by it, and commanded himself to cease at once.

The whimpering ceased. That gave him a dose of self-confidence. He retained some control over events, it seemed—some self-determination. That didn't strike him as something a fictional character ought to be capable of. Maybe he was mistaken after all. Could he be overreacting? Yes, maybe. That seemed, after all, a more reasonable possibility than what he'd been suggesting to Mrs. Chancellor. Maybe he just needed some rest. Maybe after a good night's sleep he'd wake and laugh at himself for the wild thoughts he'd entertained the day before. But it was not yet midday. Surely he wouldn't be able to sleep for hours yet. How to pass the time? He couldn't bear the thought of returning to the shop.

A book, he decided. "Reading always settles me down. That's just the thing." And he remembered he'd brought his copy of *Bleak House* home with him. Perfect. Dickens had no peer when it came to making him drowsy.

But first he would brush his teeth and change into his pajamas. It wouldn't do to wait until drowsiness took hold. Better to just allow it to take him, knowing that no business remained undone.

He brushed methodically before remembering that he'd not eaten since the last time he brushed so it hadn't really been necessary, but it made him feel better nonetheless. He peeled off his clothes and let them drop in a pile by the side of the bed, knowing his mother would have scolded him for it, but reasoning that what she didn't know couldn't upset her. The feel of his favorite flannel pajamas felt better against his skin, and he gave the discarded outerwear no further thought. Retrieving the voluminous book, he turned down his bed sheets and crawled underneath.

His eyes scanned the pages until he found the spot where he'd last stopped reading, and then he read on. An hour passed, then another. The story flowed on at its painstaking yet relentless pace. But it did its work. Elisha felt his tense muscles begin to relax, and then a welcome if intangible sensation of peacefulness. After several more chapters, the first tinges of drowsiness made his eyelids grow heavy. He willingly followed as the story led him on. And then he reached that shockingly implausible moment, the discovery of the unfortunate missing Lord Chancellor:

> They advance slowly, looking at all these things. The cat remains where they found her, still snarling at the something on the ground before the fire and between the two chairs. What is it? Hold up the light.
>
> Here is a small burnt patch of flooring; here is the tinder from a little bundle of burnt paper, but not so light as usual, seeming to be steeped in something; and here is—is it the cinder of a small charred and broken log of wood sprinkled with white ashes, or is it coal? Oh, horror, he IS here! And this from which we run away, striking out the light and overturning one another into the street, is all that represents him.
>
> Help, help, help! Come into this house for heaven's sake! Plenty will come in, but none can help. The Lord Chancellor of that court, true to his title in his last act, has died the death of all lord chancellors in all courts and of all author-ities in all places under all names soever, where false pretences are made, and where injus-tice is done. Call the death by any name your Highness will, attribute it to whom you will, or say it might have been prevented how you will,

it is the same death eternally—inborn, inbred, engendered in the corrupted humours of the vicious body itself, and that only—spontaneous combustion, and none other of all the deaths that can be died.

And that's the last thing Elisha remembered before sleep swept him up.

CHAPTER FIVE

None Other of All the Deaths

*Fire came out from the presence of the Lord
and consumed the burnt offering...*
—Leviticus 9:24

Elisha awoke to a commotion outside his bedroom window. Sounds of sobbing and frequent commands, shouted in an authoritative voice Elisha did not recognize, punctuated an indistinct background of murmuring, such as one might hear in a crowded restaurant or theatre.

The siren call of his comfortably warm bed whispered to him to linger and ignore the distraction, but curiosity proved the greater temptation, so Elisha swung his legs from under the blankets and slid his feet into the slippers that awaited them by the side of the bed. Then he reached for his robe and pulled the cord tight around his waist as he shuffled toward the window to have a look at the cause of the noise.

An unexpected and unsettling scene presented itself. All of his neighbors seemed to be gathered in the street and on the sidewalk in front of Mrs. Chancellor's house. A fire truck stood in the driveway, its engine running. Elisha noted that the shouted commands issued forth from one of its crew. Nearer to his vantage point, an ambulance had backed into his own driveway and its rear double doors stood open as if ready to receive the victim of some terrible disaster. Even as he watched, two medical technicians wheeled a gurney into view, bearing something he couldn't see under a clean white sheet. They came from the direction of Mrs. Chancellor's front door.

In an instant a sense of dread overtook Elisha. He raced downstairs and shot through his front door onto his lawn. "Wait, sir!" he called after the nearest emergency medical technician, who had just finished sliding the gurney into the back of the ambulance. The man turned toward the sound of Elisha's voice. "What, or who, do you have there?" Elisha panted. He got a sad, tired look for an answer, as if the EMT had broken more than his share of bad news over the course of an eventful career and had long since given up trying to find just the right words to make everything okay. The look gave Elisha a chill. "What happened?" he asked, unsure that he really wanted to know.

"And who are you, sir?"

"My name's Elisha. Elisha Bookbinder. I live here."

"My apologies for commandeering your driveway, Mr. Bookbinder. We didn't have time to ask permission, you understand. My name's Graham Ripper, Emergency Medical Services. There's been a... well an accident, I suppose. It's your neighbor, Mrs. Chancellor."

"An accident? How is she? May I speak with her?"

"No. I'm afraid that won't be possible."

Elisha understood. He'd suspected as much. "Well," he said, "may I at least have a look at her?"

"That's not a good idea, sir. There's not much left so there's really no point. Was she close to you?"

Elisha didn't hear the question. "What? What do you mean 'not much left'? Exactly what sort of accident did Mrs. Chancellor have?"

Ripper shifted uncomfortably. "Well, maybe 'accident' isn't exactly the right word. She's gone, that's all." Elisha waited for a more complete explanation, but the EMT seemed disinclined to offer any.

"Why is there a fire engine in Mrs. Chancellor's driveway? There doesn't appear to be a fire."

Graham emitted an audible sigh and rubbed the back of his neck. "Well, Mr. Bookbinder, it's the craziest thing I've ever seen. I mean, I've heard about this sort of thing. Who hasn't? But I always assumed it was just nonsense, you know?"

"Nonsense?" Elisha prompted, hoping Mr. Ripper would get to the point.

"Yes. But well, I guess I was wrong. Sure enough."

"In what way?" Elisha persisted, although he thought he knew.

"Look here, Mr. Bookbinder. We don't want to cause a sensation, so don't go making a fuss. But the fact of the matter is, as best as we can figure, sometime between the hours of 11:00 p.m. and 2:00 a.m., Mrs. Chancellor burst into flame, spontaneously."

A lengthy silence followed the EMT's pronouncement. The medic's face turned red, while Elisha's went deathly pale. He sensed the world starting to spin and took hold of Ripper's shoulders to steady himself. "Are you okay sir?" the EMT asked. "You don't look too steady. Maybe you'd better sit down." He guided Elisha alongside the ambulance to the passenger-side door and invited him to climb in. Elisha was oblivious to the kind gesture, as well as to Ripper's partner who sat behind the wheel filling out a detailed form. The look on the bookseller's face worried the medic.

"Her mother's name was Madeline," Elisha mumbled to himself. "She went by Maddie. But not until yesterday. Before yesterday she didn't have a name. She didn't exist. But we forced his hand. *I* forced his hand." Elisha gasped long and loud. "It's my fault," he blurted out. "And then I forced his hand again last night by reading Dickens. That has to be what's happening! Oh, how horrible! Spontaneous combustion! 'And none other of all the deaths that can be died.'"

The man in the driver's seat shot Ripper a quizzical look. Graham could see that Mrs. Chancellor's neighbor was becoming agitated—not an unreasonable reaction to learning that his next-door neighbor had died so horribly overnight—but he could make no sense out of Elisha's seemingly incoherent ramblings and wondered whether they ought to take his vitals just to be on the safe side. Before he could suggest that they do so, a change spread across Elisha's face. A look of sober resolution replaced the thousand-yard stare fixed there moments before. He spoke again, but now with dreadful purpose. "Sir, I believe I may be responsible for Mrs. Chancellor's demise."

The confession earned him a compassionate, tolerant smile. "Mr. Bookbinder, nobody's to blame. Like I told you, it was spontaneous. Nothing you or anyone else did or didn't do would have made any difference."

"But we spoke just yesterday, and I said some things that may have caused…"

"No you didn't," Ripper assured him. "It's just one of those things."

"One of those burst into flames in the middle of the night for no apparent reason things?" Elisha asked sarcastically.

Ripper smiled with patient understanding. "Yes. One of those things."

"But how can you know that I didn't do anything that contributed to this?"

"Because then it wouldn't have been spontaneous, would it? Look, her doors were all locked from the inside. There's no sign of forced entry, and no trace of a scuffle, so this wasn't done by an intruder. According to neighbors, she didn't smoke, and we've already confirmed that there were no cigarettes or matches in the house. The stove was turned off, and she had no electrical appliances running. She simply sat down in an easy chair and went up in smoke. She did have a floor lamp next to her that was turned on, but it's still completely intact. There's no faulty wiring, nothing. I've heard that in cases like this, the body is nearly entirely consumed, with next to no damage to the furnishings in the room. That's exactly what we found. I can't explain it, but I do know that no one is to blame." He patted the back of Elisha's hand reassuringly. "No one."

"Did you ever wonder what it would be like to be one of the characters in a novel?" Elisha said.

"Huh?"

"That's what we were talking about last night. Mrs. Chancellor and I. I've been, well, out of sorts lately, and Mrs. Chancellor noticed and invited me in to chat. You know, the kind of things neighbors do all the time. Except that Mrs. Chancellor and I hadn't ever really chatted before. It was the very first time I'd been in her house. Anyway, we talked about how it might feel to be a character in a story. Did you ever think about that?" Ripper admitted that he hadn't. "Some characters are central to the story," Elisha continued. "It's all about them, you might say. But others are more or less incidental. They're there for just one purpose, and once that purpose is accomplished, the author doesn't need them anymore, so he just writes them out of the story. That's how it was with Mrs. Chancellor. She came into my story just long enough for us to have one meaningful conversation, and now today, she's gone. Out of the story."

The man in the driver's seat looked up from his paperwork, and when Ripper glanced his way, he rolled his eyes. "Yeah, I guess that's one way of looking at it. And kind of comforting, in its own way," the medic acknowledged.

"Is that how it strikes you?" Elisha asked skeptically.

"Sure. I mean, just suppose that life is some sort of story. It seems to me what would matter most is not how big our part is, but whether we play it well, that we fulfill our role, even if it's just to provide comfort to an out-of-sorts neighbor. What better epitaph could she have than, 'She was there when she was needed'?"

"I suppose," Elisha agreed. "But here's the thing, Graham. After I left her place and came back home, I settled down with a book and spent the rest of the evening reading. It was *Bleak House* by Charles Dickens. Did you ever read it?"

"No. I got a small taste of Dickens when I was in school. It was more than enough."

"Well, I won't bore you with the details then. But the thing is… well there's this one part where… ah jeez."

"Where what? Go on."

"Where one of the characters spontaneously combusts." Ripper made no visible reaction to the news. "Well?" Elisha prompted.

"What do you mean 'Well'? What are you suggesting?"

"Don't you think it's an incredibly unlikely coincidence that last night I was reading about a death by spontaneous combustion, and this morning my neighbor is dead from the very same implausible cause?"

"Of course! If what you are telling me is the truth—and I can't imagine why anyone would make up something like that—then it's a startling coincidence. But that's all it is. Period. If you're trying to tell me that you caused your neighbor to go up in flames by reading *Bleak House* last night, that's just nuts. I mean, no offense but it's crazy. There's no connection. None. You didn't cause this. No one did."

"I forced his hand."

"Who's hand?"

"The Author's."

"What author? What the dickens are you talking about?"

"Never mind. I'm sorry. I'm just upset over my neighbor. Don't listen to me."

The man with the form nodded in mock agreement. "You know," Ripper offered, "we have counselors available to talk with people dealing with this sort of thing—emotional trauma, I mean. Maybe you ought to make an appointment." He reached into his breast pocket for a business card and handed it to Elisha, who took it without another word. He began to slip it into his own pocket, and then he realized he was still in his robe and grew self-conscious. He'd said far more than he ought to have, and the effect must have seemed all the more ridiculous for his gaudy pajamas and fuzzy slippers. He decided it would be best to excuse himself.

"Thank you. I'm feeling better already," he lied. "It's just the shock of so terrible a tragedy. I'll be okay once I've taken a shower and gotten dressed." He climbed out of the vehicle and smiled in a feeble effort to show Ripper that he'd recovered his senses.

"Well, I'd best be getting along too," the medic agreed. "But remember what I said. There's no use feeling guilty over this." Elisha assured him that he wouldn't, then turned back toward his front door as the EMTs resumed their paperwork. All around, once-curious neighbors were also losing interest and drifting back to their normal morning routines, leaving the public services to complete their chores while a TV news crew set up a live broadcast from Mrs. Chancellor's front lawn. That struck Elisha as decidedly unwelcome. They were bound to notice him at any moment and call him over for a sound bite about what a pleasant neighbor Mrs. Chancellor had been and how awful it was to have such a thing happen right here in the suburbs of all places. Elisha didn't relish getting dragged into a public spectacle.

They probably think they're covering the most sensational story of their collective careers, he mused. Yet all the while, he knew, they had stumbled upon something far stranger than they could possibly imagine, but remained totally oblivious to its real significance. He could tell them of course, and in doing so broadcast his theory to the world. He had only to take a few more steps in their direction and they'd surely invite him to do so. But this wasn't the right occasion. He needed time to think. Much more time. Besides, any remarks he made to these reporters would never make the evening news. They'd be edited out and saved, most likely, for the staff to watch and rewatch in their off hours, laughing amongst themselves at the expense of the crazy man in the fuzzy slippers. No, not like this. In time, people needed to know, but not this way.

Elisha ducked behind a yew tree and made for his back door, staying safely out of sight of both the news crew and the dwindling gaggle of gawkers in Mrs. Chancellor's yard. He reached the door, gave the handle a twist, and cursed his stupidity. It was locked, of course, and his key rested on his bedside table, next to the cursed lamp. Well, he had no choice. He strode quickly and deliberately back around to the front of the house. As he turned the corner into view of the news crew, a reporter called to him. "Excuse me, sir, did you know Mrs. Chancellor? Would you mind giving us a few words about this terrible mishap?" But Elisha walked through the front door and slammed it behind him without answering or even looking up.

CHAPTER SIX

The Mystery of Drew Unwin

Two men will be in the field; one will
be taken and the other left.
—Matthew 24:40

lisha wandered into the kitchen and absent-mindedly went about fixing himself some breakfast. He really ought to get a move on, he knew. The morning was wearing on, and he'd not yet showered, dressed, or eaten. He'd been at the shop little more than an hour during the previous two days, and his customers would be concerned if they found the shop closed yet again this morning. Moreover, the stove would struggle to fight off the chill if he didn't get a fire going well before opening. It was another bitter morning, colder yet than the day before when that kind Mr. Unwin had brought him his edition of Shakespeare and commented on how much he liked the shop. Elisha felt mildly ashamed of the manner in which he had hurried his guest out the door and lied to him about the reason. Not that he regretted having lied, but he felt very sorry for the *need* to lie.

The downright unspeakable events of the past twenty-four hours had shaken Elisha more than he dared to admit—the shocking epiphany, the kind invitation from poor Mrs. Chancellor, the heartfelt discussion with his neighbor, the hours of quiet tedium reading *Bleak House*, death in the night, and the shocking discovery upon wakening. Poor, poor Mrs. Chancellor. Doomed to hellfire simply because she had finished her part, spoken her last line.

Elisha didn't doubt for a moment the cause of the disaster. In one sense, Ripper had been right—no one was to blame. At least not anyone in this world. Nor did faulty wiring or a carelessly lit cigarette have anything to do with it. But it hadn't exactly been spontaneous either. Not in the ultimate sense. She had been deliberately eliminated because she'd had only one purpose, and as of the moment Elisha had stepped through her door and back outside last night, that purpose had been served. She'd done her part. Just as Drew Unwin accomplished his part in this story the moment he'd finished giving Elisha the pivotal clue to the meaning of the universe by reading from *As You Like it*.

This thought echoed in Elisha's mind, but unlike other echoes, it didn't fade out over time but rather grew stronger and louder with each repetition, until it sounded like an alarm bell inside his head. "Just like Drew Unwin!"

In a flash, Elisha realized the reason the echo kept growing in intensity was that he was shouting the words to himself out loud, his voice rising with each iteration. "Oh please," he lamented at last. "Unwin too?"

Could he possibly have survived the night? If so, he must be warned. Elisha raced upstairs and rifled through the pile of the previous day's dirty clothes, which still lay on the floor where he'd been standing while getting undressed. He found his shirt and reaching into the breast pocket retrieved the card Unwin had given him as he retreated from the bookshop. Then he bounded back down the stairs and placed a call to the telephone number on the card—misdialing once, cursing, and then starting over before hearing a ring through the earpiece. And another, and another. But Drew Unwin didn't pick up.

Elisha looked once more at the business card. Yes, it bore an address. In an instant, Elisha knew that his shop wouldn't reopen today. He began to wonder whether it ever would. Nor would his urgent mission allow time for a shower. But he would grab a quick bite, and he would get dressed before leaving the house again.

Not ten minutes later, he set out to search for Unwin. But first, he peeked through the blinds of his living room window and saw no sign of the news crew. The ambulance had left too, but the fire truck remained in Mrs. Chancellor's driveway. Elisha prayed it would not cross his path again all too soon, at Unwin's house this time. Might he too be reduced to a smoldering heap of ashes awaiting discovery by some unfortunate neighbor, or by Elisha himself? It seemed quite possible to him as he climbed onto his bicycle. And how about Graham Ripper? How interesting it would be to hear his reassurances that, yes, two spontaneous human combustions on the very same evening within ten miles of each other certainly made for an odd coincidence, but nothing more. Just one of those things!

Elisha strapped on his helmet and pedaled off toward the address he'd already memorized. Within moments he realized that, thankfully and quite unintentionally, his hastily chosen course of action provided just what he most needed. Whatever he might find upon arriving at Unwin's residence, the bracing morning air against his exposed face invigorated him. Riding had always restored his soul, even while it taxed him physically. He enjoyed both sensations equally and counted them among the greatest pleasures his simple lifestyle afforded him. He considered himself fortunate that he could enjoy them on a nearly daily basis. He treasured the blessed memory of the day he had first learned to ride, setting in motion a lifelong habit that yielded innumerable occasions of genuine bliss. There was, after all, much to be said for the simple life. Perhaps that's what really mattered in the end, he speculated, not whether the blessings were "real" in some metaphysical sense, but what we made of them, and how much we enjoyed them while they lasted. Because they never lasted very long, did they?

The question brought his mind back to Unwin's possible fate. The hope remained that he might knock at the bookseller's front door to find him contentedly reading from *As You Like It*, and that he would explain apologetically that, yes, he had heard his phone ring but he'd been in the shower and just hadn't gotten around yet to returning the call. Elisha prayed it would be so, but he didn't count on it. This trip of his could have only two outcomes, he reasoned. He might find Unwin dead, thereby confirming his fear that becoming an unnecessary part in the Author's story led to fatal results. If, on the other hand, he found Unwin safe and sound and entered into a conversation it would not disprove his theory, but merely demonstrate that Unwin's role remained unfinished after all. Could he save Unwin's life, he wondered, by making a constant daily nuisance of himself so that the man's part in the story never ended? Or would that be an even worse fate? "There's no use getting ahead of myself when I don't even know where I'm going," he scolded himself. "Better to just see what there is to see at Unwin's place before worrying about what it means and what to do next."

Elisha's heart raced as he neared his destination, whether from the physical exertion or in anticipation of what he would discover he couldn't say. Upon arriving at the correct address, he drew encouragement from the fact that the front door stood ajar. Surely Unwin would not have left the door open the previous evening upon retiring for the night, so someone must have been wandering about the house earlier this morning. That offered good hope that the bookseller had not shared Mrs. Chancellor's fate.

He rang the doorbell, but heard no response from inside the house. After a few moments, he called through the partially open door. "Hello? Are you there Mr. Unwin? It's Mr. Bookbinder. From the bookshop. I spoke with you yesterday, and I'm hoping we might talk some more today. Do you have a moment?" He waited for a reply and again heard nothing. His high hopes began to fade, but he hadn't ridden so far to give up easily.

Growing bolder, Elisha pushed the door farther open and stepped inside, feeling foolishly conspiratorial. By this time, he didn't know whether he'd be more discomforted to find a man-shaped smudge on the living room carpet or a perfectly healthy homeowner outraged by Elisha's uninvited presence. The room before him was unoccupied. Everything seemed in its place, with a single exception: Unwin's copy of *The Works of Shakespeare* lay on the floor, opened to the very passage that had set the events of the previous day in motion.

Elisha superstitiously chose not to touch it. Instead, he stepped over it and continued on through the dining room and into the kitchen. He found no signs that a meal had been prepared that morning. The dishwasher stood empty. The trashcan contained a clean plastic garbage bag, but nothing else.

Retracing his steps, Elisha returned to the living room and headed upstairs, where he discovered neatly made beds in each bedroom. When he guiltily peeked into a dresser drawer, he found an orderly pile of stacked shirts. He wandered down the hallway and into the bathroom. The towels all felt dry to the touch, as did the shower. A full roll of toilet paper hung by the side of the commode. Elisha looked out the bathroom window and onto a freshly mown but deserted backyard. A large pile of quicklime sat conspicuously just outside the back door. Otherwise, the entire residence had not so much a well-kept appearance as an unused one, as if it and its contents had been shrink wrapped until moments before Elisha had arrived. Of its owner, Elisha found not the slightest trace.

At a loss, Elisha sat down on the front stoop and turned what he'd discovered over in his mind. There seemed no reason to suppose anything drastic had befallen Unwin, but neither anything to explain his absence. It struck Elisha as strange and yet vaguely reminiscent of something he couldn't quite recall.

One thing seemed certain. No one had spontaneously combusted in this house. If Unwin returned here after visiting Elisha, he'd departed again, willingly or otherwise. Yet if their fates diverged, in several other ways he and Mrs. Chancellor shared strangely similar stories. Neither had played a substantial role in Elisha's life. Each had occupied center stage for but a single day. Both had been influential in leading him to conceive and then articulate a radical new worldview. Could there be some deeper significance to these facts or were they simply, as Graham Ripper would say, coincidental?

Elisha wracked his brain, hoping to find some clue that would explain how these people had been connected to each other and to him. "What else? What else did they have in common?" he wondered aloud. Mrs. Chancellor seemed somehow tied to the events he'd been reading about in *Bleak House*, but not Unwin, to his own good fortune. So the similarities ended there.

But wait! That wasn't entirely true.

Unwin too had a link to the novel, didn't he? Not in such an apocalyptic fashion as Elisha's neighbor, to be sure. The connection seemed so trivial that Elisha had nearly forgotten, but now memories of the previous morning came over him in a torrent. Unwin had gotten lost in the fog! Of course! That was a clue! He'd been late because he'd driven right past the bookstore in the morning fog. Hardly a momentous turn of events, and that explained why Elisha hadn't taken it into account. But at the very moment Unwin had missed his destination in the mist, Elisha had been reading in *Bleak House* about "Fog on the Essex marshes, fog on the Kentish heights. Fog creeping into the cabooses of collier-brigs; fog lying out on the yards and hovering in the rigging of great ships; fog drooping on the gunwales of barges and small boats."

Yet something still didn't line up. Yesterday's fog definitely pointed to *Bleak House*, but it failed to explain Unwin's disappearance. No one he'd read about since yesterday had vanished without a trace. Nevertheless, the persistent sensation that Unwin's disappearance seemed like a story he'd heard somewhere before returned, stronger than ever. Try as he might, he couldn't connect the dots. Time passed.

With a sigh, he stood once again. He suspected he'd learn nothing more here, and a growing desire to put some distance between himself and the home of a man whose mysterious disappearance suggested foul play put an end to his ruminations. He had no desire to encounter a neighbor and be forced to explain why he'd felt at liberty to wander uninvited into the home of a man he'd met only once, or why he'd come here in the first place. To remain any longer would be to invite ruin, and luck was a commodity he'd never had in great supply. Happily, Unwin's house sat back from the street, and both shrubbery and distance shielded it from even the closest of his neighbors. Elisha felt sure no one had yet taken notice of his presence. Still, it was time to go. Remounting his bicycle and pedaling more slowly than on the outward-bound leg of his trip, he began the ride back home.

Once again, the cold December breeze on his bare face swiftly did its welcome work, refreshing him like a cool drink on a hot summer's day. Intent concentration, he realized, could be as draining as physical activity, and it felt good to rest his tired brain and instead put his muscles to work. He found himself wishing the half-hour ride back home would take longer and considered making an unnecessary detour to prolong his pleasure. The world looked different from the seat of his bicycle, and he considered the new outlook an improvement. Somehow, he saw things more clearly from the saddle. That applied equally to the world around him and to the workings of his own mind. Some people, he knew, could concentrate only when given total silence. Others found silence oppressive. For Elisha, neither alternative constituted the ideal. He did his best thinking while outdoors on his bike. And so before long, clues that he'd unsuccessfully chased while sitting on Unwin's front step began coming to him unbidden.

He realized, first, that he was not as dumbfounded by Unwin's absence as he ought to be. Consciously he had expected to find Unwin, either dead or alive, in his home. But subconsciously, he somehow sensed that it made perfect sense that he should be missing. Why should that be? And why did everything he found at the house, despite being decidedly odd on the natural level, feel somehow right and proper in his gut? He felt almost as if things had to be just the way he found them.

It came to him next that it wasn't the first time that morning he'd felt that way. He'd been distraught, he remembered, to learn Mrs. Chancellor's fate, yet not entirely surprised. That tragic scene, too, had a verisimilitude to it. Almost as if he knew it would happen. But that was easier to explain. He'd been reading *Bleak House*. His own experiences had been replaying the literary scene from the night before. It had been like watching a rerun. He'd seen it before and knew what to expect, in some degree, at least. But not with Unwin. No one in *Bleak House* had disappeared without a trace. So why did these events, too, seem like a rerun? That's a mystery, Elisha thought.

And as soon as the word entered his mind, the mystery solved itself. "Mystery!" Unwin's disappearance was not tied to *Bleak House* after all, but rather to *The Mystery of Edwin Drood*, the novel Elisha had read years before, and by rights, according to the rules of his own little game, he should have begun reading again yesterday while waiting for Unwin to arrive at his shop. *Bleak House*, in point of fact, had been a cheat, a misguided effort to thwart fate. Edwin Drood, Elisha remembered, had disappeared in the eponymous unfinished novel, just like Drew Unwin. Elisha knew then that he had seen the last of his unfortunate customer. He would not return.

CHAPTER SEVEN

Frightening Responsibilities

Then he said to them all: "If anyone would come after me, he must deny himself and take up his cross daily and follow me. For whoever wants to save his life will lose it, but whoever loses his life for me will save it.
—Luke 9:23–24

As soon as Elisha arrived back home, he trudged upstairs and sat on his bed to remove his shoes. He had more thinking to do, but his legs needed a rest, so he'd have to do it out of the saddle and from the next best place, his shower. He let the water run while he undressed so it would be piping hot when he got in under the spray. By then, billows of steam filled the room, and he couldn't help thinking once again about London fog and Dickens and his long-neglected bookshop. Again today it would remain closed. He'd begun thinking of his once-beloved workplace as a dangerous vortex where just about anything might happen—and happenings of late had seldom been good. He resolved also to avoid any more reading of any sort until he worked out the nature of the causal relationship between his books and his physical reality, if indeed such a relationship truly existed.

He pondered, too, another side to what he had learned through the fates of Mrs. Chancellor and Mr. Unwin. Might this strange nexus between fictional worlds and his own provide him with a method of communicating with the Author of his own, personal story? To Elisha, it went without saying that the Author could send messages into this world. In fact, this world amounted to nothing more nor less than the Author's revelation, through and through.

He writes us all into existence, Elisha reasoned. *We* are *his message. All of history as we understand it is his message to some unimaginable audience.*

He wondered whether he could possibly make contact. If by reading *Bleak House* he had somehow given the mysterious Author the idea of writing Mrs. Chancellor out of the story by spontaneous combustion, that implied that Elisha could influence how the story unfolds, certainly on an unconscious level and perhaps more intentionally. If even the mere thought of reading *Edwin Drood* could make Unwin vanish without a trace, then could Elisha somehow make the Author appear? Or would even the attempt be irresponsible? Who could predict the result? In the wake of this morning's events, Elisha felt a frightening responsibility to use his discovery wisely and with considerable restraint. What horrific consequences might follow from simply picking up a newspaper and glancing at an article detailing some ghastly crime? Or worse yet, reading a history of some great battle? Yes, he resolved, he'd have to keep a short rein on his thoughts. It wouldn't do to put any more dangerous ideas into the Author's head by daydreaming.

But another possibility gave him cause for hope and even excitement. If he could potentially wreak havoc with undisciplined thoughts, didn't it also follow that he could carefully direct his musings in such a way as to lead the Author to write peace, love, or lots and lots of chocolate into his story? A verse he'd learned in Sunday school came to mind: "Finally, brothers, whatever is true, whatever is noble, whatever is right, whatever is pure, whatever is lovely, whatever is admirable—if anything is excellent or praiseworthy—think about such things." Could he incite good deeds merely by thinking about them? Possibly. But wait, had he ever really been to Sunday school, or was this memory, like that of learning to ride his bike, newly made to fit this moment in time? Yes, he tended to suspect that it was. The Author must be at it again, he imagined, and somehow Elisha was a part of the process, his every thought meshing with the Author's like some sort of dance that the Author was leading, but which Elisha followed and reacted to.

The feasibility of sending thoughts back up the line and into another world demanded careful consideration. The associated risks couldn't be taken lightly. He shuddered when he remembered the carelessly glib manner in which he had encouraged Mrs. Chancellor to ask provoking questions about learning to ride his bike in order to "force his (or her) hand." He determined to try no further such experiments until he'd weighed the possible outcomes. Fools rush in, he knew, and a conviction was growing within him that he was no fool, that this implausible-sounding idea of his had roots in reality. The cost of proving that had been two human lives.

Elisha supposed that the Author must possess virtually unlimited power and be capable of erasing memories or deleting years of his life at will. Suppose he (or she?) didn't like the tone of Elisha's voice or his train of thought and edited the past month of his life out of existence without a moment's hesitation or remorse? Elisha recalled the numerous times he had taken a stab at writing, only to quickly lose interest. He replayed in his mind's eye his callous habit of dragging his unfinished text files to his laptop's trash can icon and thus wiping them from existence. What must that have been like for the crudely crafted characters in those unfinished yarns?

Did they feel themselves dissolving into nothingness? Elisha couldn't begin to say and hoped never to learn the answer. A horrible fate, it seemed to him, even if they'd felt no pain—worse even than poor Mrs. Chancellor's. At least she'd left behind some traces, even if they amounted to nothing more than ashes and a few fragments of bone. But imagine being so thoroughly obliterated that you left behind not even the slightest memory that you had ever existed—to pass unfinished, unlamented, and unremembered. Surely that wouldn't be his own fate. He simply couldn't risk doing something that would so offend the Author that he deep-sixed this entire world and started over with a new project altogether. Elisha held the fate of the known universe in his hands. The responsibility loomed too large for him to bear on his own.

But who could he possibly enlist to offer support and guidance? No one else even suspected the true nature of their world. If they learned, it might drive them more than half mad—certainly not the right sort of mind-set to entrust with such delicate diplomacy between two parallel worlds.

The only two people Elisha could easily imagine might have been receptive to his idea had already dropped out of the story. There had to be someone else he hadn't yet thought of. Or so Elisha believed, at least. Every well written story included all the necessary characters. Otherwise the plot would grind to a halt. For Elisha's plan of communicating with the Author to work, the Author himself (or herself) needed to be a willing participant, and if he (or she) was willing he (or she) would have to write someone into the story to play the part of helping Elisha pull it off. So he didn't really have to find the right someone, he decided, he merely needed to recognize that person when he (or she) came along.

Elisha felt encouraged. For what seemed like the umpteenth time that day, he wracked his brain, replaying recent events in his mind and mentally listing everyone he'd already encountered who might fit the part. As with so many questions, the answer seemed obvious once he'd thought of it. He sprang from the shower and ran, dripping and naked, downstairs to the kitchen trashcan, and fished out the business card he'd tossed there yesterday—the one given to him by Graham Ripper: "We have counselors available to talk with people dealing with this sort of thing," Ripper had said. "Maybe you ought to make an appointment."

Elisha read the card: "Horatio Huxley, PsyD, Clinical Psychologist. Professional counsel when a friend is not enough. Available by appointment only. 555-452-8900."

Elisha closed his eyes, took an especially deep breath, and then dialed the number.

"Dr. Huxley's office," said a pleasant female voice, "how may I help you?"

Elisha thought it prudent to be circumspect, so he asked, "May I speak with the doctor, please?"

"Are you an existing client or is this a referral?"

"A referral, I suppose. I was given Dr. Huxley's card by an EMT yesterday. He suggested that I call. You see, my neighbor died under rather strange circumstances and—"

"Hold please."

Elisha heard a click and then soft music replaced the melodious voice. After a brief pause, another voice came on the line.

"Mr. Bookbinder? This is Doctor Huxley."

"How did you know my name?" Elisha asked with some alarm. "I never told the receptionist who I was."

"No worries, Mr. Bookbinder. I was told you might be calling. It seems one of the first responders who handled the, uh, call this morning is worried about you. He told me you seem to be taking your loss hard, so I'm glad you called. I'm here to help you work through this. Why don't you come in and tell me what's on your mind?"

"About Mrs. Chancellor's accident, you mean? Or—"

"About anything you want to get off your chest. I'm just here to listen. That's what I do. I listen."

"Because I don't really want to talk about her. Well, that is to say I do, but not just about her. It goes far beyond that. There are other things I need to share with you. I need your help."

"I know you do. That's why I want you to come in. Are you seeing anyone else? A specialist, maybe?"

Elisha could tell he wasn't making himself clear. "No, you don't understand. I mean I want you to help me answer some questions. I've been trying to work something out, and I need someone to help me decide what to do."

"Please, Mr. Bookbinder, I don't want you to do anything until we've had a chance to chat. Will you promise me?"

"Of course, but—"

"Are you free tomorrow? It's best not to let these things wait."

"'These things'? Doctor, this isn't something you're likely to have heard before. You see, I've been—"

"I know you have, but we'll set all that to rights, I promise. There's nothing to worry about. I'll see you tomorrow at 1:30 and you can tell me all about it. Remember, I'm here to listen."

"This is will be worth your time."

"Yes, yes, Mr. Bookbinder. If you need directions, press '1' to talk with the receptionist. Otherwise I'll see you tomorrow."

"No sweat. I'll be there." Elisha hung up the phone, wondering what Horatio Huxley might have thought had he known that the man he'd been listening to was stark naked. He picked the phone up one more time and ordered a large pepperoni pizza before putting on fresh clothes. He didn't want to have to leave the house again. He needed to recapitulate recent events and work on his presentation if he hoped to win Huxley's confidence. Tomorrow would be an important day, and he was determined to prepare for it in advance.

CHAPTER EIGHT

Clever Word Games

Their idols are silver and gold,
made by the hands of men.
They have mouths, but cannot speak,
eyes, but they cannot see,
they have ears, but cannot hear,...
—Psalm 115:4–5

Elisha talked for quite some time without the slightest interruption from Huxley. In fact, without so much as a nod or even a raised eyebrow. Elisha assumed nothing from the doctor's loud silence. He simply took full advantage of it to give voice to his ideas, subjecting Huxley to the fullest, most well-reasoned presentation he could offer for his startling new worldview. For nearly an hour he spoke, almost breathlessly, building the case for his theory piece by piece. He'd once heard that if you can't clearly articulate an idea, then you don't really understand it, and so he found himself pleased by the cogency of his confident and unfaltering oration. As he drew ever onward toward his conclusion, he felt he had indeed constructed an unassailable defense of his thesis.

"And so there it is, Huxley," he concluded. "This world is make-believe. And we're all just players—you, me, poor Mrs. Chancellor, everyone."

Elisha felt elation mixed with relief. All along, as during the conversation he'd had with his unfortunate neighbor, Elisha feared that his confidant might burst out laughing. He hadn't, but neither did he seem pleased. On the contrary, after listening to Elisha in silence, Huxley seemed agitated. If Elisha had to guess, he'd say that the doctor appeared to be suppressing a sob.

Collecting himself, Huxley found his voice and took upon himself the task (he thought it an altogether necessary and noble one) of trampling Elisha's theory underfoot, fully intending to obliterate it before it led to dreadful consequences of a sort he could barely begin to image, but which he instinctively feared.

"Now look here, Elisha," he ventured, "it just won't do. Your premise is wholly unsupportable. Do think. Let's suppose—only for a moment, mind you—that what you say is true. If we're just characters in a story, that would mean that somewhere—I can't begin to imagine where—there has to be an author. And he's deciding all of the events of our lives. Isn't that so?"

"Yes, precisely," Elisha acknowledged. "Although I'm not sure the author is a man. He may be a woman. Or *she* may be, that is. I mean, since I seem to be the protagonist, it's probable that the author is a man too. That seems most natural. Though I freely admit that a woman might also choose to make her lead character a man. At least, I don't see any definitive reason why she couldn't. After all, Agatha Christie created Poirot, didn't she? And Dodgson created Alice." No sooner had Elisha said so than he kicked himself. No good could come from tempting the Author with references to such potentially dangerous works as murder mysteries and *Wonderland*, he scolded himself.

"Either way," Huxley continued. "If we're in a story, then some-one, be it a man or a woman or a creature from Mars, must be writing the story. And if there's an author, then we're not in control of our own destinies. Everything that you or I say or do would be bound to the whim of the author. We'd be mere puppets, unable to think for ourselves or to act contrary to his tyrannical machinations. That is to say, it's his plot, and we could have no say in how the story unfolds."

"Why so?"

"Well, there's just no way around it. It's common sense. Think, Elisha. You're a lover of books. Have you ever once, while reading a book, had one of the characters speak to you? Maybe tell you that he's tired, so please stop reading so he can take a break and get some rest?"

"Not so far," Elisha responded cagily.

"Of course not. Because storybook characters have no free will. They have no initiative. So if we were in a story, how could you possibly discover that fact unless the author intentionally revealed it to you? You don't claim that he's spoken to you, do you?"

It was a thought Elisha had not yet considered. He half wished that the author *had* spoken to him directly, just so he could triumphantly counter Huxley's jest. But on the other hand, he was grateful he could truthfully assure Huxley that, no, he hadn't yet heard any voices inside his head.

The truth was, until now, Elisha had remained uncertain whether his discovery pleased or terrified him. At times he almost wanted to be talked out of his new conviction, to be shown some fact he'd overlooked but which conclusively refuted his thesis so that he could resume his workaday life without further care and have a good laugh at himself for his gullibility. Yet now that Huxley held his idea up to critical thought, he found himself growing defensive. He felt his face grow warm.

"No, he hasn't spoken to me. Or she hasn't. But don't you see that your reasoning doesn't work? Characters in a story never talk back, you say. They never know they're not real. But how can you say what storybook characters really think about? Maybe they have good reasons of their own for not speaking up and revealing the truth. And after all, all you can do is draw inferences from how characters behave in the books you and I have read in our world. But if I'm right, the story we're in isn't a book of that sort at all. It's something different. It's written by someone living in a whole other world, an uber-world that might be governed by altogether different rules from this one. The Author stands outside of our world, so he may not be governed by the same reality."

"But see here," Huxley countered. "You talk of this so-called author as if you've already proven his existence. You've done no such thing. You're simply speculating. There must be a hundred and one more plausible reasons for these strange feelings you say you've been having. A soaring imagination strikes me as the most likely.

"Listen to me. You love to read, yes?" Huxley postulated. "Of course you do. And you have a special affinity for fiction and drama, am I right? You're always deep into the novels of Dickens, or the plays of Shakespeare, or as you say, Dodgson." Elisha shuddered at the reference and cursed his stupidity for having mentioned the name in the first place. "Suppose you've got it all backwards? Suppose you're not really the pawn of a mysterious unseen author who's dictating all your thoughts and actions. Maybe *you* are the author! Novels and plays have filled your head with all sorts of fantastical ideas. You admire many of the characters you read about. Subconsciously, you envy them. You want to be part of a tall tale and have great adventures, just like them. So now you're unconsciously fulfilling that wish by conjuring up ideas about unseen worlds where imaginary authors work to create, well, us. Can't you see that your ideas are nothing more than wishful thinking? Therefore, you can't accept any of them as real."

Elisha was unimpressed. "It may or may not be real," he admitted, "but it can't be dismissed that easily. It's all wishful thinking, you say? Well, I say that your rebuttal is no less so. If you reject anything that we find attractive on the grounds that it must be wish fulfillment, then neither should I accept your own theory, because it seems as attractive to you as mine does to me. You can't believe in the Author until his existence is proven, you suggest. Well, I put your argument to the same test. Can you prove it?"

Huxley sighed. "Elisha, please. Do be sensible. You're not thinking."

"On the contrary, Huxley. I've not stopped pondering the evidence since I began to understand the truth. This isn't just some crazy notion. Well, I admit it was at first, fair enough. If I had confided in you yesterday or the day before, you might have found it easier to talk me out of this." Huxley wished it had been so and mumbled something to that effect, but Elisha ignored him. "No longer. I've examined it rationally. I've already asked myself the very same questions you're asking. I've wrestled with all of them, and the more I do, the more answers I discover, and the more sensible it all becomes."

"Well, of course it does," Huxley allowed. "Don't you see that only proves it's a red herring? You want it to be true because it provides a comforting explanation for your..." He paused, not wanting to be unkind. "Well, your fantasies, I guess. So you're convincing yourself that it makes some kind of logical sense. But it doesn't. Trust me, dear Elisha. You can, you know. I want nothing but the best for you. Why else would I have listened to your story so patiently? And why else would I be giving you such sound advice?"

"You've made a good life for yourself. A bit on the sheltered side, it seems to me, but all in all a good life. You don't want to become an object of ridicule, do you? I don't want to see you lose the respect of your customers, or worse yet, lose your business altogether."

Elisha admitted, though only to himself, that he'd gone in fairly short order from being appalled by his discovery and wondering where it might lead him, to more than half wanting it to be true, and finally, just now, to being afraid it might be false. What did it say about his real motivations that he could buy so easily into so improbable a proposition? Might his eagerness to believe make him a mark for every huckster with an unsold bottle of snake oil? Huxley could easily be right about the consequences of being proved a fool.

On the other hand, proving himself right would only be the start of his troubles, not the end. The pitfalls of being correct outweighed any foreseeable benefit, as far as Elisha could yet foresee. His knowledge came with grave responsibilities. No, all in all, Huxley's interpretation didn't hold up. Elisha's ever-growing conviction could not be attributed to simple wish fulfillment.

"Again, your own reasoning betrays you," he retorted. "You say I want this to be true so I'm deluding myself into believing it. But what about you? Clearly, you want it to be false. Maybe you're the one who's delusional. Maybe you refuse to accept the truth because it means you'll have to admit you're not in charge of your own life. Maybe the idea of being your own self-made man is so intoxicating that it blinds you to the truth—the truth that you're just the opposite of all that, a product of someone else's imagination and that apart from him, you're nothing. Quite literally nothing. Maybe you feel threatened and are in denial.

"Maybe you simply don't like the idea that there might be things you'd enjoy doing but never will, simply because the Author hasn't written them into the story. A month-long Hawaiian vacation maybe, or an affair with a gorgeous celebrity. Maybe you resent the fact that he (or she) hasn't given you a more glamorous part, so you just refuse to acknowledge his existence. Or hers."

Elisha noticed that the color had drained from Huxley's face and knew his counterthrust had struck near to the doctor's heart. But the psychologist fought on bravely, saying, "Hardly. I just don't believe in anything I can't see and touch, that's all. If it's not physical, it's not real."

"Do you really think so?"

"Absolutely."

"Yet you can neither see nor touch psychological theories, so by your own logic, they can't be real."

"You're missing the point."

"How so?"

"You're muddling the issue with clever word games. But you can't deny the common sense behind what I'm telling you. It goes without saying. No, I can't prove it, but it doesn't need any proof. It's self-evident. Some things you just have to accept on—" Huxley stopped, realizing he'd been trapped and wondering how he hadn't seen it coming.

"On faith?" Elisha offered.

"On rational deduction," Huxley countered. "On the irresistible principles of logic."

"Which you've likewise never seen nor touched. Yet you do not doubt their validity. Indeed, you've based your life and your career upon them, and now you're urging me to do the same—to trust in something you can't touch or prove. But really, Huxley, if faith is what you are selling, I have no need for the principles of logic. I already have a conviction I can't prove to be true, but which nevertheless compels belief. I have faith in the Author. So your principles of logic are quite superfluous."

Another sigh from Huxley. "The difference, as you are well aware, Elisha, is that my principles of logic are time-tested and scientific. They've proven themselves to be reliable in a multitude of circumstances. They have a solid record of helping people overcome doubt and reaching sound conclusions. To that extent, they have in fact been proven. No, not mathematically, but practically. And it's practical truth that really counts in the end. Not abstract speculation of the sort you're engaged in."

"What could be more practical than discovering who we really are," Elisha wondered out loud, "and why we're here? I mean, if there really is an Author and he's telling a story, then what is he saying, and to whom? What themes is he expounding upon? How do our actions contribute to those themes? Are we free to either hinder or help his purpose? And if we are, then should we? Are his intentions honorable or nefarious?"

Elisha realized he was talking more to himself now than to Huxley. He hadn't fully articulated this side of the question until now. Yet he sensed that he'd at last hit upon the real crux of the issue. If he was right, if all the world was simply a stage, then what was this whole drama leading up to? It might be a comedy, wherein all turned out well in the end and all wrongs were put right and everyone, not least the protagonist, lived happily ever after. But he had no reason to suppose this was the case. Take poor Mrs. Chancellor. Spontaneous combustion seemed an unnecessarily cruel fate. If her part of the story had really come to an end, couldn't the Author have chosen to have her move to Chicago to live out her days in peaceful anonymity? But no. She'd been incinerated. It had to mean something, didn't it? But what?

And if this story was a tragedy, then what? Maybe he and everyone he'd ever met or known was racing toward inevitable destruction, helpless pawns in the hand of a Writer whose only concern was using them to make some inscrutable moral point, after which he didn't really care how their part in the story might end. Worse yet, might he be caught up in a mere potboiler aimed at no better purpose than making money? Or worst of all, what if the Author was an existentialist! The sort of destiny that might await him in that case simply didn't bear thinking. Was he heading toward being and then nothingness?

Elisha began to perspire profusely. The walls seemed to be closing in around him, and he felt a distinct sensation of being cruelly trapped in a place of someone else's choosing. He realized, to his surprise, that Huxley had been talking at him. He was just now wrapping up some hastily contrived point about living in the here and now or some such thing. But Elisha no longer had any interest in what he said. He'd come seeking affirmation but had found only more questions. Answers, he realized, could not be found here. Huxley had none. Or rather he had none that led anywhere. He had only excuses for going nowhere.

"Elisha! Are you listening? What's gotten into you?"

But Elisha was already halfway to the door.

"Don't forget!" Huxley called after him. "We have another session together same time next week!"

CHAPTER NINE

King Herod on Steroids

When King Herod heard this he was
disturbed, and all Jerusalem with him.
—Matthew 2:3

E lisha considered foregoing his plans for the evening in favor of sequestering himself away in his bedroom in order to work through the troubling question of the Author's motives. But no, Christmas Eve had arrived, and weighty though the question remained, it could wait for twenty-four hours while Elisha gave thought to his many blessings and thanked the Blesser by taking time to worship. Besides, he'd been too long without some sort of emotional refreshment. The anxieties he'd wrestled with had occupied his mind continuously for days, and he'd begun to feel rather like a drowning man who faced a bad end if he couldn't get his head above the water sooner rather than later. Church seemed like a good place to take a breath. It would do him good.

He rifled through his closet and found something smart but comfortable to wear and plenty warm. The church stood just a few blocks from his home, and he thought it would be pleasant to walk there. That way he could enjoy some time alone with his thoughts on his way to the service. With any luck, maybe he'd be able to draw some conclusions before entering, and in that way be better able to relax and get into the spirit of the holiday. If so, it would be well worth the inconvenience of struggling to flip the pages of his hymnal with numb, stiff fingers.

Before stepping outside, Elisha chose a long scarf, mittens, and a woolen cap, and bundled himself against the chill. It felt safe inside his several layers, as if in addition to keeping out the frost, they might protect him as well from all the dangers and uncertainties of a world that had so recently been turned upside down. He liked the sensation. He stepped through the doorway, headed down his driveway, then turned left toward the church. The brightly decorated houses lining both sides of the street cast a rainbow of colors onto the sidewalk before him. Somehow, even his darkly brooding thoughts about Unwin and Mrs. Chancellor seemed less oppressive in their glow.

"Poor Mrs. Chancellor," Elisha thought to himself for what must have been the hundredth time since her passing. She had enjoyed the Christmas season more than any other time of the year, and her excitement, much like that of a young child's, was infectious. He'd miss her dearly. Did it have to be this way? He'd asked himself the question before, but more or less rhetorically. Now he really wondered. The answer, if only he could arrive at it with any degree of confidence, would in turn settle other, even bigger questions about his mysterious Author's motivations. He knew that if he put his mind to it, he might easily come up with a handful of possible scenarios in which Mrs. Chancellor's death served a larger purpose—in the same way that a firefighter who sacrificed his own life to save a helpless infant trapped in a burning house could be celebrated for an act of selfless heroism. If similar ideals motivated the Author, then perhaps Elisha should cooperate so as to help him achieve his ends. Or her ends, Elisha reminded himself. But supposing that any such thing lay behind Mrs. Chancellor's sacrifice would be hard to prove.

The alternative, of course, was almost too frightening to consider, but no less likely. Perhaps the Author had no regard for the welfare of his characters and disposed of them quite carelessly whenever crafting some more congenial fate proved too tiresome. He might even take sadistic pleasure in making people suffer. In that case, might it be possible to oppose him and thereby thwart his designs? It seemed implausible, Elisha had to admit, but the gravity of the question demanded that he at least ponder the possibility and if it proved to be feasible, to act on it.

But which was it? Were the Author's motives honorable or nefarious? So much depended on the answer. Elisha felt that to act in any manner without having a handle on the answer would be foolish, if not to say potentially disastrous.

He turned one more corner, and the church came into view. Bright white headlights and fiery red tail lights in the parking lot added their luster to the yellow candlelight streaming forth from the pastor's study and the kaleidoscope of liquid color coming through the beautifully backlit stained-glass windows of the sanctuary. The bright smiles on the faces of arriving worshipers completed the cheerful scene. Elisha took heart. At this time of year, and on this night in particular, miracles could happen. He believed it. Maybe an epiphany awaited him. He prayed it would be so.

As he approached the entrance, a young couple just ahead of him turned and, seeing him hurrying toward them, held the door for him. "Merry Christmas!" they intoned on cue. Elisha knew he'd hear the phrase mindlessly echoed many times before the evening ended, yet it nevertheless sounded good to him, and he cheerfully returned the same greeting. Taking a program from an elderly gentleman wearing a necktie that read "Wise men still seek Him," he entered the sanctuary hoping to find a seat toward the back, but the room was filling quickly, and the best seats were taken, so he had to wander more than halfway to the front before he found a place to sit—on the far outside aisle, at least.

He sat and glanced at his program. "Use the time before the service begins to reflect in silence on the Christmas story and its meaning for you," he read. That seemed to imply that Christmas had more than one possible meaning, Elisha thought, and that we were free to choose one that suited us. He wondered whether that was really so. He thought not. Truth was truth whether it pleased us or not. He half-wished it were otherwise, because he feared what truths he might discern about his Author. But even if such fears were realized, it was manlier to face the implications bravely, look inconvenient truths in the eye, and stare them down rather than to live forever in deluded self-denial. Or so he believed.

Elisha reflected all right, but his own story fully occupied his thoughts, leaving no room for cogitations on the Nativity, which seemed distant and foreign to him at any rate. The fates of Unwin and Mrs. Chancellor, on the other hand, affected him personally, and their meaning seemed to hold a higher priority, even on Christmas Eve. He briefly wondered whether coming here had been such a good idea after all, but even as he did, the service began with the choir inviting everyone to stand and join them in singing, "O Little Town of Bethlehem," one of Elisha's favorite carols. By the time they began the second verse, his thoughts had fully returned to the reason for the season and he felt renewed contentment.

As the final verse reached its conclusion, the Reverend Preston Johns stepped to the podium, invited everyone to sit, and read the opening Scripture passage: "After Jesus was born in Bethlehem in Judea, during the time of King Herod, Magi from the east came to Jerusalem and asked, 'Where is the one who has been born king of the Jews? We saw his star in the east and have come to worship him.' When King Herod heard this, he was disturbed, and all Jerusalem with him."

How inscrutable, Elisha thought, that a single event could elicit two such diametrically opposed responses. To some, it represented a much-anticipated blessing and a cause for rejoicing. For another, it elicited a sense of danger, posed a threat to the established order, and validated a need for preemptive action. The opposing outlooks could not both be valid. Two incompatible conclusions never can. But how could the people of that time know which path to take? It seems so obvious after the fact. But suppose Herod had been right to fear the Christ child? Might he be remembered as a hero, rather than the villain of the story?

Elisha could not help but sympathize with the king's dilemma, for he shared it. He was no prophet. He was King Herod on steroids. He had to fathom the Author's intentions based on pitifully few facts, as well as evaluate the probable outcomes, draw a conclusion, and then act on it, perhaps irrevocably. Might he be judged as harshly as Herod if his responses proved equally faulty? Elisha found himself wishing for a good deal more wisdom than he knew himself to possess, in order to figure this puzzle out. And yet he'd never heard that even the wisest of men in this or any previous age had ever suspected the truth he alone had deciphered. If he alone among all the great thinkers throughout the years had unraveled the truth, could he really be so witless? Could it be that his own wisdom rivaled that of the Magi, and that there was no one better equipped to make the critical choice than he?

Even if that was true, wisdom could only accomplish so much. Suppose that like Herod, he decided that the Author was a threat. Could he intervene any more effectively than Herod himself had done? It didn't seem likely. It appeared that he could exert a limited influence on the Author. But he had no reason to believe that he could compel the Author to do anything he didn't consent to, let alone prevent any action that he favored. Elisha and the Author inhabited two different worlds. Or greater still, two different realities. And of the Author's reality, Elisha knew nothing. How could he make any rational choices whatsoever on that basis? Every assumption he might consider would eventually run into an event horizon beyond which he could never see. Dead ends all, doomed by the depths of a profound ignorance to lead nowhere. And no one else, be it the philosophers, the scientists, or the theologians, could possibly know any more than he did.

Elisha realized with a start that the congregation was standing and singing again, leaving him conspicuously disengaged. Feeling a rush of embarrassment, he fumbled for his hymnal, then consulted the program to learn what page he could find the words on, and rose just as the music ended and everyone sat back down.

Elisha too returned to his seat while the pastor began his homily. "Brothers," he said, reading from Paul's letters to the Corinthians, "think of what you were when you were called. Not many of you were wise by human standards, not many were influential, not many were of noble birth. But God chose the foolish things of the world to shame the wise. God chose the weak things of the world to shame the strong."

He appeared to have his eyes fixed on Elisha while he recited the passage, and Elisha had no doubt the words were meant for his ears. "He who has an ear, listen to what the Spirit says to the churches." The pastor continued, but by then, Elisha was paying no attention. The words already spoken filled his mind. They seemed to be written just for him and just for this moment—a revelation. They supplied him with both an answer and a course of action. They told him he could never be smart enough to unravel the Author's motivations under his own power. No one ever had been. Human wisdom simply wasn't up to the task. It merely got in the way of the truth. If he were ten times smarter, that would only make him ten times less likely to understand. "The right tool for the right job," he'd always said. And it was true. Wisdom, he now realized, was not the right tool for this one. This puzzle required something else altogether. Something quite the opposite. Elisha now knew exactly which tool he needed. What's more, he had it in his toolbox. He'd been using it all his life and had gotten quite good at wielding it.

From the pulpit, the pastor offered some heartfelt encouragement that Elisha missed. When several of the congregants replied with shouts of "Amen!" Elisha too, overcome by the epiphany he'd just experienced, shouted "Amen!" but for entirely different reasons. His mind raced, spurred on by excitement now, rather than concern. His course, he realized, would not be nearly so tortuous as he'd first imagined. It was not up to him at all to judge the author's intentions. How could he? Even if he were somehow able to know the Author's every thought and every motivation in infinite detail, how would that qualify him to say whether those thoughts and motivations were ethical? Water can't rise higher than its source, so how can a creation ever presume to judge its creator, or to rate his own ethics as superior to those from whom they derive? No, wisdom cannot pass judgment on ethics. It's a tool intended for quite a different job and useless for the purpose he had foolishly tried to apply it to. But the right tool was readily available. It lay within arm's reach. The right tool would seem foolishness to others, Elisha knew, but he didn't care. He knew it was exactly what he needed. And rare and underutilized as this foolish tool had become in the world he inhabited, he, at least, had it in spades and was well practiced in its use.

Things that might never yield to study become clear in the more gentle light of humble submission. The answers he sought, the Author already possessed. If he only trusted his Creator to answer his call, all would be made clear. There was nothing to fear. Nothing but his own pride and suspicions. Nothing but the absurd belief that he might possibly understand his world better than the one who had created it—that he might choose a purpose for himself other than the one that was being written for him. Nothing, be it wisdom or foolishness, could thwart that purpose other than his own stubborn insistence on deviating from it. No answer he found could ever be correct if it did not conform to the unsearchable will of the one who defined correctness. And if that one chose to remain hidden, then hidden he would remain. Indeed, if the one looking for answers relied only on his own wisdom and refused to look beyond himself, in that case too the inventor of wisdom certainly would remain hidden. The answers, Elisha knew, lay beyond the boundaries of his world, in a place he could never hope to go. Well then, he'd humbly wait for the answers to come to him. How that might happen or what it might look like he couldn't imagine. But that too was a question pointless to consider. If the Author wanted it to happen, he'd find a way. If he didn't, well then that was that and no sense fussing over it.

Elisha was glad he'd come to church. Christmas was all about new hope, and that's exactly what he'd discovered. He was satisfied. But the service wasn't over yet. The pastor, unaware that his message had already produced a profound change in Elisha's outlook, droned on: "Your attitude should be the same as that of Christ Jesus: Who, being in very nature God, did not consider equality with God something to be grasped, but made himself nothing, taking the very nature of a servant, being made in human likeness. And being found in appearance as a man, he humbled himself..."

"Yes," Elisha agreed. "A servant. That's what I'll be. I'll wait. And while I wait I'll listen. Then we'll see what is revealed."

CHAPTER TEN

In the Flesh

I was hungry and you gave me something to eat, I
was thirsty and you gave me something to drink,
I was a stranger and you invited me in.
—Matthew 25:35

Elisha slept late the next morning, Christmas day. Normally, he spent the holiday at home alone and counted that a present to himself. He rarely took days off, and doing so on Christmas made the day special in a way that festively wrapped packages couldn't match. This year, to be sure, Christmas was the fourth consecutive day since he'd last opened his shop, but tradition was tradition, and he still looked forward to spending the day alone, so he had made no other plans.

His bedside alarm clock read 9:00 before he finally rose, put on his fuzzy slippers, and wandered downstairs. He retrieved two eggs from the refrigerator, turned on the stove, and waited for a frying pan to get hot. While it did, he dropped two slices of bread into the toaster and poured himself a glass of milk.

The telephone rang. "Who the dickens could that be?" he muttered aloud to himself. He cracked his two eggs into the frying pan before answering. Then he picked up the handset and noticed that the caller ID read "UNKNOWN."

"Hello?"

"Merry Christmas, Elisha," an unfamiliar but friendly voice said. "It's been a long time coming, hasn't it?"

"Three hundred and sixty five days," he replied dryly. "Forgive me, but who is this?"

"Someone with answers to your questions. Well, most of them anyway. I've been keeping an eye on you, Elisha, and I know what you've been wrestling with. I know your secret. What's more, I know that you are right about a great many things. You're wrong about a few, too, but as far as the big picture, you're on the right track. You're very perceptive, really. It's been interesting watching you, but up till now, I've kept myself at a distance. Now I think it's time we met. I'm hoping that if I drop by, you'll invite me in. I guarantee it will be to our mutual satisfaction. So what do you say, may I visit you?"

Despite the caller's seemingly helpful offer and kind voice, Elisha felt all warmth leave his body to be replaced by the sort of terror one might feel if he heard a high-pitched scream while walking through a graveyard—a fear of something at once deadly, beyond all understanding, and entirely inescapable. Elisha felt naked and vulnerable. How much more did this caller know? He had undoubtedly been snooping, unseen and unsuspected, for days. For him to now politely ask for permission to visit struck Elisha as sheer mockery. Clearly he was able to get or do anything he wanted, regardless of whether it suited Elisha's pleasure or not, and was perfectly willing to do so.

"Elisha? I know you're still there, and I know you can hear me. And I know this call is unsettling. But trust me, please. I want to help you. I have things to say to you, things you need to hear. You won't be sorry, I promise."

Elisha couldn't begin to imagine anything appropriate to say, so he simply hung up. An instant later, the phone rang once again. It took him till the third ring before he gathered enough courage to pick it up, but still he couldn't think of anything to say, so he merely put the speaker to his ear. "Elisha, listen. This is the last time I'll call. If you really don't want to hear from me, I'll understand. But then you'll never find what you're looking for. The choice is yours, but please don't be hasty. A good deal hinges on what you decide. So which will it be? Shall I leave you alone?"

Strangely, Elisha found it much easier to answer "No" to this question than it had been to give assent to the previous one, even though both answers amounted to the same thing.

"Good!" the caller exulted. "I'll see you shortly. Why don't you put another couple of eggs on the stove. We can talk over breakfast." And the line went dead. At a loss for what to think or do, Elisha obediently grabbed two more eggs from the fridge and popped two more slices of bread in the toaster.

By the time he had finished setting the table for two, he heard a knock at the door. He padded out into the living room and, curious over what he might be getting himself into, took a furtive peek through the blinds. A middle-aged man stood on the front step, and even as Elisha peered at him, he raised his arm and knocked again. He stood a shade under six feet tall, Elisha judged, and wore casual clothes, maybe even a little overworn, as if he had no interest in impressing anyone with his appearance. His hair was gray and not too recently trimmed. He looked like someone who didn't get much exercise, but he had a pleasant bearing about him overall. Elisha felt slightly reassured by what he saw. The man appeared simple enough and harmless.

Bracing himself for he knew not what, Elisha opened the door. "Good day, Elisha." The stranger beamed. "Thank you for seeing me. I know this is uncomfortable for you. May I come in?"

Elisha nodded and took a step back to make way for his visitor. The man smiled and entered.

"Ah!" he exclaimed as he came inside. "I can smell breakfast. Wonderful! I'll tell you what, Elisha, why don't we sit down, and I'll do my best to explain who I am and what I have to say. In the meantime, you may simply call me Christopher. It's as good a name as any."

For reasons he couldn't explain, his guest's manner put Elisha at ease, and the uncertainty he'd felt since answering his phone melted away. "Follow me, and allow me to serve you."

"Perfect!" Christopher chimed, sounding as though he approved of the way the encounter had begun. He followed Elisha into the dining room. "You have a nice home here. It strikes me that it needs a little more work, though." Elisha couldn't be sure exactly what that meant, but somehow it didn't feel as though Christopher intended it as an insult.

"I've often thought myself that it seems unfinished," Elisha agreed. He motioned for Christopher to take a seat while he fetched two plates each piled with scrambled eggs and a pair of sausage links. "What would you like to drink? Coffee?"

"No, thank you. I don't have a taste for coffee. Some orange juice would be fine. I believe you have a carton on the top shelf of your refrigerator."

Elisha stopped short. The sensation of dread returned. "How do you know that?"

"A very pertinent question, Elisha. And one that I fully intend to answer. But first, it might not be a bad idea for you to have a seat." Elisha did so immediately, without taking his eyes off the stranger in front of him. "Let's enjoy our breakfast while I talk," Christopher suggested. This will take a good bit of time and otherwise this fine meal will be cold before we can enjoy it."

"Go ahead," Elisha offered. "I think I'd rather listen."

Christopher looked mildly disappointed. "Well, as you wish. As to the orange juice, your question provides me with the perfect starting place for our chat. By the way, are you going to go get it for me? You did offer me a drink, after all." Elisha felt foolish and wondered whether the whole conversation would be this way, meandering down many pathways without ever getting to a distinct destination. Nevertheless, he opened the refrigerator door, took the orange juice from the top shelf, and fetched a glass before returning to the dining room. He placed both the carton and the glass on the table and then sat down and began eating his meal, forcing his guest to pour his own drink. Elisha knew it was petty, but it seemed necessary to demonstrate that he retained some small degree of control over this appointment.

Christopher didn't seem the least put out and helped himself to the juice. "As I said," he went on, "your question about how I knew you had orange juice in your fridge is more profound that you realize, although the answer itself couldn't be simpler. I knew it was there, you see, because I put it there."

Elisha's cold stare said a thousand words. Christopher continued, "Well, in a manner of speaking, that is. But essentially, that's just what I did. Let me explain, Elisha—although, you already know the explanation, don't you? You stumbled upon it yourself several days ago." He paused, giving Elisha a chance to catch up. Slowly, gradually, his host's eyes grew wider. "Yes, I can see that you're beginning to comprehend." He chuckled in a friendly way. "Elisha, you were so flummoxed by me knowing the contents of your refrigerator that it never occurred to you that you can't remember buying this orange juice. Think. You don't remember it, do you?"

Elisha shook his head slowly, thinking that this was probably just how Mrs. Chancellor had felt the morning he had asked her to remember her mother.

"Of course you don't. It never happened. The carton wasn't there until just a few moments ago when I first mentioned it to you. I created it for just one purpose—to convince you who I am. I apologize for unnerving you, but there's just no better way to show you that what I'm saying is true."

Elisha understood. A sense of the uncanny filled him, something halfway between fear and awe. "You're the Author, aren't you?" he rasped in something between a whisper and a shout.

"Well, now that's a question even more profound, but less easily answered than the last one," Christopher replied. "On the one hand, it would be very correct to say, 'Yes I am.' But on the other hand, I could tell you, 'No, I'm not' and it would be equally true. So which would you rather hear?"

"Please, I want to hear both truths!" Elisha exclaimed. "I've been doubting my sanity and living in fear of what people will think of me when I try to explain that we are all just players. Tell me everything! Tell me in what ways you are the Author and in what ways you are not. I want to hear! I can't imagine how both can be true at the same time, but if they are, I want to understand how it *can* be, and why it *must* be."

"Well said, Elisha! Do you see now that you can trust me?" Elisha assured him that he did. "Good. In that case, you are ready to hear about the Author. But first, I'll need to tell you who *you* are and what this world that you live in is really like. I warn you, it might be a little humbling—although you've guessed parts of it already. The Author has been leading you toward these discoveries bit by bit, so that you'd be able to cope with it once you've learned the whole truth."

"You mean how none of us in this world are real?" Elisha interrupted. "That we're just characters in a story?"

"No. It's not so bad as that. Yes, you are a character in a story, as you have guessed. So is everyone you've ever known. But it doesn't follow from that that you are not real. Quite the contrary. You are as real in your world as the Author is in his. It's simply that your reality is of a different nature than you ever dreamed before just a few days ago.

"Being in a story doesn't make anyone any less real. It just makes you, well, it makes you kind of small. At least in comparison with the Author, I mean. Now don't get me wrong. Small doesn't mean unimportant. I don't mean that at all. Some of the most important things of all are little—children, for example. And you. And this world that you live in. You are all quite important. You have a reason and a purpose—a big one. One the Author needs you to accomplish on his behalf. But while your purpose is big, your world remains small in the physical sense.

"You've probably heard all your life about how large the universe is, right?"

"Sure," Elisha admitted. "I mean, I can't even begin to imagine it, but I know it's really humungous big. Big enough to hold billions of galaxies, each of which contains billions of stars."

"That's right," Christopher concurred. "But only from your own point of view. For the Author, things are different. For the Author, your entire universe fits onto the hard drive of his laptop computer, with plenty of room to spare for video games."

"That's awfully small," Elisha allowed.

"Humbling," Christopher specified. His host nodded. "I'm not telling you this to belittle you, Elisha. You asked me whether I am the Author, and I am simply trying to explain to you the differences between his world and yours so that you'll understand who I am."

"So you're really not the Author after all?"

"No, I'm not."

"Then who are you?"

"Well, you see, one reason the Author can't just turn up on your doorstep like I did is that he wouldn't fit into your world—this world he created. If your whole universe can fit onto his laptop, how could he possibly fit on your doorstep?"

"It would be a tight squeeze, I suppose."

"Very tight. And between the two of us, he's not in any shape for it. He's just as chunky as I am. He has trouble fitting into his jeans, let alone into a tiny little universe like yours."

"That makes sense, I suppose."

"So if he somehow wanted to pay you a visit, he'd first have to find a way of shrinking himself quite a bit. Cut himself down to your size, you might say. If he could do that, well then your world just might be big enough to handle him."

"Wonderful!" exclaimed Elisha. "But is there a way? Can it be done?"

"As a matter of fact, there is, and it can. In a manner of speaking at least. But size is just one reason the Author doesn't fit easily into this world. Size matters, to be sure, but there's an even more fundamental problem that comes between you and him. And I'm afraid this one is even more humbling than the first. Are you ready to hear it?"

Elisha was.

"In addition to being small, your world is barely tangible. You don't notice it because you're a part of it and therefore, no more substantial than any other part. People in your world like to say that unless they can touch something and feel it, they won't believe in it. Well, the truth is, compared with the Author's world, this one barely exists. It's more of an idea, an abstraction, than you probably want to believe. That doesn't mean it isn't real. But it does mean that it's of an altogether different quality than the Author's world. So even if he could fit, you couldn't really experience him in a satisfying way. It would be like a ghost trying to embrace a living man. It doesn't work, because a ghost is hardly there at all. There's just not enough of him, you might say. Or if that's too macabre for you, it would be like trying to arm wrestle a hologram. A literary personage like yourself may have every feature and faculty that people in the Author's world do—eyes, ears, hands, legs, speech, you name it—but although you are real, it's a different kind of reality. I know that's hard to picture. But think of it the other way round. What if you tried to enter into any of the stories you've ever read and talk to one of the characters? How would you do it? Where could you even begin?"

"I see your point." Elisha sighed. "It would be impossible."

Christopher laughed. "No, Elisha, you don't get my point at all. I'm not telling you that it's impossible. I'm telling you it can be done. And now I'm going to tell you how."

CHAPTER ELEVEN

Farther Back and Higher Up

Your attitude should be the same as that of Christ Jesus:
Who, being in very nature God,
did not consider equality with God something to be grasped,
but made himself nothing,
taking the very nature of a servant,
being made in human likeness.
—Philippians 2:5–7

"Go on! You have my attention, Chris. I'll admit I was scared half out of my wits when you called, and then again when you asked to come here in person. I didn't know whether you were a stalker or a con artist or what. But I want to know more. Please don't stop. Tell me how the Author can enter this world, and whether he intends to do so."

"You may rest easy on that score, friend. His arrival is at hand. It's really not all that complicated. I'm sure you'd unravel it yourself if you had the patience to think it all through. The problem, as I've tried to explain, is that the Author can't fit into your world himself, and that even if he could, he'd be of such a nature that the two of you could not possibly interact as equals. But think. What is it that the Author does best? He creates characters. He imagines storylines and lives and then brings them into being. So all he needs to do is create one more literary character to add to those he's already created—one into which he puts all of his own foibles, ideas, purposes, and dreams. And then he introduces that character into the story. Because he is a literary character, he could relate to you on your own level, and in your universe. But because the Author put himself wholly into that character, he could speak on the Author's behalf, and share all the insights and creativity of the Author himself. And that, dear Elisha, is who I am," he finished.

Elisha jumped to his feet. "So you are the Author after all!"

"Yes," Christopher answered, "I am. Peace to you on whom his favor rests."

Elisha pondered the significance of the words. "So do you mean to say… Is the Author of my story God?"

Christopher laughed out loud, but not in an unkind way. "No, Elisha, it's not so good as that, I'm afraid. We're not God. Not by a long shot. To find God you'd have to go farther back and higher up. We are merely subcreators—writers—and not among the best, I'm sorry to say. You've noticed that yourself. You told me that your home feels unfinished. Other aspects of your life do as well, I know. Some of that was intentional. We used it to get you thinking along certain lines you needed to consider. Ones you wouldn't have pondered had your life been more polished. But I confess that other parts of your life seem unfinished because our talents aren't quite as refined as we'd like them to be. That's why we borrow ideas from the works of better writers, like Dickens, and although you haven't yet noticed, C.S. Lewis and Tolkien. That's just one of the consequences of having someone less capable than God in charge of creating worlds. It's a deuce of a job. We've been at work on your story for a very long time, although in your world it appears to have occupied just a few days."

"I'd have thought it was the other way around—that a thousand years in my sight would be as a watch in the night to the Author."

"Sometimes it works that way, but not always. Time is a funny thing, and not nearly as predictable as you might think. It's virtually impossible to draw any conclusions about time in one world based on how quickly it passes in another."

Elisha considered that. It puzzled him that it should be so, but he anticipated that no matter how many more questions he asked, Christopher would be unable to state things more clearly than he already had.

"Very true," Christopher responded, although Elisha didn't recall saying anything. "But you have other questions that can be answered more profitably. Now's the time. I'm here to instruct you as best I can."

"But won't we be sidetracking the story? I mean, whatever this tale is all about—and I can't say that I've figured it out—aren't you keen to get on with it and carry it to a climax? Especially if you've already been working at it for as long as you say. I would imagine such a scene as you are suggesting would bog things down considerably. In fact, as much as I appreciate you entering into my story in this manner and answering questions for my benefit, it seems like rather poor style, with all due respect."

"And so it would be," Christopher agreed. "If this story was about anything other than what it is."

"Which is?"

"It's about this very moment. This conversation isn't getting in the way of the climax. This *is* the climax, Elisha. Well, one of them anyway. There will be another."

"So all these questions I've been pondering, they are my purpose?"

"They point to your purpose. Every character needs purpose. So far, your whole life has been leading up to this. But this is also just a beginning. Soon it will be up to you whether or not you complete your purpose."

"Up to me? But is it really? If this story is being written for me, how can I walk any other path than the one you choose for me? Are you saying that I have free will? I don't understand how that could be so."

"Nor do I know how to explain it to you. But it's true. This story has taken a very different course than we envisioned when we first set out. There are certain limits you can't go beyond, of course. If you deviated too far from our primary intent, we'd have to rein you in. But you have more say in how this tale unfolds that you might think. You've taken on a life of your own, Elisha. And we've been happy to make adjustments to the plot in response to your feedback."

"Feedback?"

"That's about as well as I can explain it. Again, we're just subcreators so it's only in our power to grant you so much freedom and no more. For more, you'd have to go farther back and higher up. Only the Prime Mover can do that."

A prolonged silence followed while Elisha sorted out everything he'd heard to this point. Christopher waited patiently, allowing him all the time he needed to sift through the bewildering revelations and assimilate them. Elisha pushed food around his plate with a fork as he ruminated, knowing what the next question had to be but uncertain as to whether he dared give voice to it. "Don't be afraid to ask, Elisha," Christopher said softly. "Remember, that's the whole point of this scene. You can't offend me."

"So this is my purpose?"

"It points to your purpose, as I said. Revelation is never an end in itself. It must lead on to something more tangible. It must elicit a response. If it doesn't, then the story can't end. It would go on forever, leading nowhere, and never getting there. Every story needs a point. Otherwise, it would be pointless."

"And how about Mrs. Chancellor? Did she have a purpose too?"

"Everyone has a purpose, Elisha."

"What was hers?"

"Now that question, my dear friend, is the least profound one you've asked so far. You don't need me to tell you the answer. You already know it."

"Well, I think I do. Are you telling me that I'm correct, then, in believing her sole purpose in life was to give me someone to whom I could expound my theory? That seems pretty passive, hardly a purpose at all."

"Some roles are dramatic, Elisha. Others are mundane. Hers was of the mundane sort. But that didn't make her any less vital to the story. How else would readers know what your revelation in the bookshop entailed? It was a critical stage in setting up this very moment. And she played the role beautifully. What better way to be remembered than as one who fulfilled her purpose?"

"But then why such a gruesome end? It seems a strange manner of thanking a useful character who only did what she was crafted for."

"I assure you that it wasn't. She didn't feel a thing. And her death actually helped move the story along to its next essential moment. It gave you a reason to rush off in search of Mr. Unwin."

"But why kill her at all? Even if she's spoken her last line, couldn't her life have gone on uneventfully for as long as the story lasted?"

"Everyone must have a purpose. To linger on beyond all purpose and meaning is not to live, but only to rot. Besides, she's not gone. It only seems that way to you. But to readers in our world, she lives forever. Every time readers open the pages of this story and begin to read, they'll find Mrs. Chancellor at home in her kitchen cheerfully baking cookies and lending an ear to her agitated but kind-hearted neighbor."

"Oh. I guess I never thought of it that way."

"Most folks never do."

"And Unwin?"

"What about him? The same principle applies. I needed him to give you the key clue that unlocked the secret of your universe. He played his part as masterfully as Mrs. Chancellor. So he won't return. You won't see him again in your story, but he's already attained immortality by virtue of just having a part in it, though a small one. As long as the story endures, so will he. What could be more congenial? Of course, as you say, we could have just had him move to Syracuse or Peoria, but where's the fun in that? Making him disappear without explanation is so much sexier, don't you think? There's a danger, you know, when writers begin to take themselves too seriously. They become boorish."

Elisha considered this. "So you can inject whatever sort of crazy happenstance you like into my story, regardless of whether or not it conforms to physical laws or contradicts something you've already written?"

"Well, technically that's true," Christopher conceded, "but that would be bad writing. We try to avoid that. Events are just like people. All of them have a definite purpose too. We don't add anything just because we can. At least not in stories written for adults. Adults like it when everything follows the rules, and they get testy when things don't conform to expectations. It's different with children's stories. Youngsters will gladly accept whatever you tell them without question. It's a much healthier attitude, and it makes them more receptive to really clever tales and really important lessons. Of course, there's a danger too. You can't tell them any lies or be less than completely honest with them. If you do that, you turn them into adults in short order—always doubting, never trusting, rarely believing. In both your world and ours, that happens all the time. It's why adults have a hard time with the really important truths. They've been fooled too often in the past and now they just can't accept anything that's not self-evident, and even some things that are. I don't need to tell you that. How many adults so far have you been able to convince of your discovery? How many have you even dared try to explain it to?"

"Not very many," Elisha conceded.

"There's time for that. After all, it's not your purpose to convince anyone in your own world of what you've learned."

The statement surprised Elisha. "You keep saying that this conversation fulfills my purpose in part only. What exactly remains to be done?"

"You'll have to figure that out for yourself, I'm afraid. I'll only say that a choice is coming for you, and I need you to do the right thing. It's frightfully important in my world that you do. But don't worry. You're coming along just fine so far. I'm confident you'll get it right."

"And when I'm finished, will I disappear from the story too, like Unwin?"

"No. When you accomplish your purpose, the story ends. Does that frighten you? It shouldn't. It's the best of all possible destinies. Really wise characters long for it and work toward it."

"I don't suppose you can tell me whether the end is near?"

"No. Not because I don't want to, mind you. I simply don't know. We're making good progress, but as I've already told you, how it all unfolds is largely up to you, so it's hard to predict. A lot hinges on this very conversation, for example. Until it draws to a close, I'm not exactly sure what comes next."

"Is it coming to a close?"

"Yes, it is."

"What remains to be said?"

"An excellent question!" Christopher exulted. "And again, it's one you know the answer to, if only you realized it. The answer, ironically enough, is another question. Another profound one. One you need to ask me. One no one else can answer. If any other character could have answered it, I wouldn't have had to enter your story in such an overt way. As you know, this really isn't the normal manner of storytelling. But in this case it was necessary. So ask away."

Elisha felt a tinge of panic arise in his soul. He sensed that he faced a critical moment, and that much depended on asking the intended question—the pertinent one that the entire story hinged on. He felt certain it was his destiny to ask it, but despite Christopher's assurance, he didn't believe he knew what it was. He wondered how he could stall for time.

He glanced across the table toward his guest, but without looking into his eyes. Christopher seemed in no hurry. He finished the last of his eggs and emptied his glass in a manner that suggested he might wait patiently for the rest of the day if that's how long it took Elisha to ask just the right thing. But all Elisha could think of was, "Would you like another helping of eggs?"

Christopher looked up in sudden amusement and then laughed into his napkin. Elisha felt his face grow warm with embarrassment as he realized what he had done; then, he too snickered at his own expense. "Our talk has gone better than I had hoped, Elisha. Don't be embarrassed. This too is a matter of some importance, I grant you! But allow me to make this easier for you—on two counts, no less. First, as to the question of more eggs, yes, thank you very much. I would gladly have another serving. But I'll help myself, if you'll permit me, so that you needn't leave the table."

Elisha realized that his visitor's plate and glass were both full once again. "Being a character of my sort has its privileges, as you can plainly see. When I have a mind to, I can put food on my plate as easily as I can put juice in your refrigerator. And now let me help you once more. You see, not only can I put juice in a refrigerator and eggs on my plate, I can also place thoughts into your head. I believe that if you search there once more you'll find the key question waiting for you, because while I certainly could wait all day for you to think of it on your own, I choose not to."

CHAPTER TWELVE

It Is Finished

And being found in appearance as a man,
he humbled himself
and became obedient to death—
even death on a cross!
—Philippians 2:8

Elisha searched his consciousness for the new thought and found it waiting for him, just as Christopher had said. Still he hesitated. He didn't want to seem difficult, but he wondered exactly how much depended on how his interview unfolded. "What happens if I don't ask you your question?"

"But it's not my question. I know the answer. The question belongs to you. Now the answer, that belongs to me. But I'll give it to you if you ask me."

"And if I don't?" Elisha persisted, noting that Christopher had neatly sidestepped the issue.

Christopher shrugged. "Then you don't. It's not what I am hoping for, but we'll write our way around it somehow. There's always a way. We call them 'rewrites,' or 'edits,' or 'second drafts.' They're a nuisance, but a necessary one. It has taken quite a few already to reach this point in the story. If it takes a few more, so be it. It will easier on both of us if you ask the question so we can get on to the next chapter, but it's not imperative. Be prepared to live with the results of your choice, but if you chose to be stubborn, it's up to you."

Elisha wondered if that was entirely true. He doubted that he had as much say over the course of things as his visitor implied. "Couldn't you just force me to ask it?"

"Naturally. But that's not why I'm here. I'm here to partner with you, not to overpower you. The fact is, I could write this story entirely without your cooperation or even your presence if push came to shove. But then it wouldn't be the same story. It wouldn't be *your* story. It would be something altogether different, and that's not what I want. I want you to be a part of it—a big part—and the only way you can do that is by accepting the role I've given you, making it your own, and accomplishing your purpose." He smiled playfully. "But now we're getting very close to answering the key question after all, aren't we? So why don't you just go ahead and ask it?"

And so Elisha did. "Does the Author have a purpose?"

A look of profound pleasure lit up Christopher's face, and he sat up straighter. "More than one," he replied, through another mouthful of eggs. "First, he has what I'll call an immanent purpose. He's fulfilling this purpose through me, right now, here in your dining room. It's a purpose contained entirely within the scope of this story and bound by it. The immanent purpose is my own particular *raison d'etre*. It's what I'm here for. It's very similar to the purposes served by Mrs. Chancellor and Mr. Unwin. You see, there are certain things that need to be revealed as the story unfolds. Each one of us has been written into the story at a particular time and place in order to disclose some necessary information—or in some cases to give you the opportunity to disclose it—and thus advance the plot. And just like Mrs. Chancellor and Mr. Unwin, I will very soon have fulfilled that purpose. Once I do, you'll see me no more." Christopher paused, as if he were choosing his next few words with particular care. "My own exit will be rather dramatic, I'm afraid. Rather more so even than Mrs. Chancellor's. You might not want to be watching so as not to upset yourself."

"For heaven's sake!" Elisha exclaimed. "I think you've already upset me! Do you mean to say you're planning another gruesome death and for yourself this time? Whatever for?"

"In this case, it's necessary to reassure you once more that what happened to Mrs. Chancellor is no cause for excessive grief and certainly not evidence of a sadistic tendency toward cruelty. I know, of course, that you've wondered about our motives. It seems to us that willingly enduring a similarly unconventional demise presents a fair opportunity to convince you of our good intentions and to demonstrate that it's not the end of the world, only the end of this chapter. Of course, the manner of my departure is not entirely crucial to this particular story, but I like you, Elisha, and it pleases me to offer this little demonstration on your behalf. Only remember what I said about looking away. I wouldn't want my final scene to make a bad impression. That wouldn't be neighborly."

"Good heavens! I don't know what to say!" Elisha exclaimed, as he tended to do when he didn't know what else to say.

"Then don't say anything," Christopher suggested. "I assure you that it's not necessary. It's more important for the moment that you listen. If you recall, I said that the Author has more than one purpose. So far, I've only told you the first of these—the immanent purpose. He also has what I'll call his transcendent purpose. That one's a little grander and harder to explain. But if you keep the immanent purpose in mind and use it as an analogy, I'm sure you'll catch on.

"This second purpose is transcendent because it is, as I said earlier, farther back and higher up. The Author is not God, I told you, but only a subcreator. He is, in fact, a creation himself, very much like you and I. Only whereas you and I are the product of a rather modest subcreator, the Author is a creation of the Prime Mover—the creator above all subcreators. That makes him a good bit more… well, more substantial, for lack of a better word. Still, he too is in a story—one that his Creator has fashioned around him. A story that is also one step farther back and higher up than yours. Just like you and I and every character in any story, he has a purpose in his own higher and farther world that's not quite the same as his purposes in this one—although they are distant relations, you might say. Do you follow?"

Elisha wanted to say that it was quite possible to follow someone and still be lost, but he decided against it. "I'm not sure," he admitted. "You would know better than me, I suppose."

"True enough," Christopher granted. "Still, it's not the same as hearing you give voice to your thoughts. It brings life to your role. Never depend entirely on the Author to speak for you. Expressing yourself in your own words is a part of your purpose. Even if what you say flows directly from the ideas he's given you. Speaking them makes them your own."

"Then what I believe you are telling me is that the Author was created for a purpose, and that his purpose in creating me was to somehow fulfill that original purpose. Is that it?"

"Excellent! That's it exactly! You see, Elisha, there are times when a character in a story can explain something better than one could explain it to people in his own world. You just demonstrated that wonderful truth. And you will go on demonstrating it for as long as this story lasts."

Elisha frowned at the thought of his story reaching a conclusion. He remained unconvinced that reaching the end would work to his own advantage. "Will I see the end coming before it arrives? Will I have any warning that my time in this story is up?"

"That's not for you to know," Christopher responded. "That's not why I'm here. Besides, any answer I might give you would be misleading. I already told you that time works funny when you jump between worlds like I have. The moment at which the story concludes for you will not be the same as the instant it ends for the Author, and both are different yet again from the time at which a reader would say, 'Now it is over.' And yet all things do in fact come to an end. It's sad, but necessary. If today never ended, then tomorrow could never begin. People never seem to take that into account. Except authors. They get it."

With that, Christopher rose abruptly and announced, "And now, my own time is nearly over. I must be going. But before I do, I believe you have one more question that you would like to have answered. It's time that you asked it."

Elisha spoke without hesitation. "How can I convince the people in my world of everything I've learned this morning?"

"The answer is that you cannot. You have not been given that ability, I'm afraid. That would take the story in a direction it was never intended to go. And now I must reveal something that you will find hard to accept: You will have to tell them nevertheless."

Elisha agreed. It was hard to understand, let alone embrace. "But why? It seems insidious to leave me with an impossible task and yet hold me accountable for doing it."

"Now, now, Elisha. That's one more question than I've permitted you to ask," Christopher noted patiently. "That one you'll have to reason out by yourself. It would spoil everything if you were to learn it too soon." Elisha was nearly certain he noticed a gleam in his visitor's eye and a slight but undeniable hint of a smile overshadow his face as he said, "You have a hard path to walk, Elisha. If it were otherwise, it wouldn't serve its purpose. Anyone can walk a road paved with gold, and many do, but there's a road less travelled, and few get to see what lies at its end. Are you at all curious where it leads? We'll see. But in the meantime, remember what I've told you about my exit. I'll say my goodbye here in the dining room and see myself to the door. You needn't follow. In fact, once I'm outside, you won't be able to. Goodbye, Elisha. Thank you for the wonderful meal. It's been a true pleasure meeting you. We are very pleased."

With that, he turned and walked through the living room and out the front door, closing it behind him. Elisha watched, transfixed to where he sat by the weight of everything he had just been told. Never in his life had he been quite so aware of the gravity of the choices he faced. And more than that—by the choices he'd already made, and would continue to make. Already the next of these bore down on him. What in the world should he to do now? On the one hand he felt that the dramatic revelations he'd been entrusted with called for some decisive, definitive action, but he'd just been told that broadcasting this revelation would produce no results. Christopher had said that his visit represented a climax of sorts, but he'd also implied that Elisha had quite a bit of work ahead of him—a hard road. So was his story nearing an end or not? How to tell? One thing only seemed certain: he'd need to tell someone, or maybe several someones, about the revelation he'd received. How and under what circumstances he didn't yet understand, but he hadn't gotten the impression that Christopher felt it to be urgent. Elisha rather understood it as something he'd be fated to do now and then, over and again, as occasion demanded, for the rest of his life. What was it that the Apostle Peter had written? "Always be prepared to give an answer to everyone who asks you to give the reason for the hope that you have." But was that what Elisha had? Hope? He honestly wasn't sure.

So rather than act on anything he'd just heard, or even think any more about it, he choose instead to fetch the morning newspaper from the driveway, where it would by now surely be laying. The decision seemed utterly inconsequential, and therefore it pleased him greatly. There would be plenty of time later on for momentous choices.

He stood, strode across the living room, and without further thought, opened the door Christopher had closed just moments before, heedless of disregarding his visitor's warning. When he did, he noticed that his guest had not gone far. He stood motionless in the street just outside, arms extended to each side. At that very same moment, out of a cloudless sky, a lightning bolt crackled across the heavens and touched the base of a utility pole across the street. The wood splintered, and the pole began to fall. For just the briefest moment, it stopped at a slight angle, held back by the tension of four overhead power lines, two attached to each arm of the crossbar at the top of the pole, but these withstood the strain for only a split second before snapping, whereupon nothing remained to prevent the pole's fall. It smashed into the street, or almost. Christopher's body prevented it from impacting the macadam. An expulsion fuse pierced one outstretched arm, a surge arrester the other. A severed wire whipped through the air and somehow wrapped itself several times around Christopher's head, while two others lashed his back. Then there was silence. The pole lay flat against Christopher's broken body, from behind his bloody head, down the length of his spine, and on between his legs to a spot just inches from where it had once entered the ground. Christopher uttered no cry of pain, nor gasped for breath, nor moved any of his crushed limbs. His part in the story was unmistakably finished.

Elisha stood unmoving and even strangely unmoved for quite some time, until he heard a distant siren begin to wail, faintly at first but growing ever louder and more shrill. He sat on the door-step, knees close to his chest, hands folded on top of them, staring vacantly at the sight he'd been clearly warned more than once not to look at. Yet he didn't feel the horror Christopher had cited as the reason for turning away. Instead, he felt a kind of stoic resolve—a resolve to do something he couldn't yet fathom.

A flashing light caught his eye as emergency vehicles of assorted shapes and sizes turned the corner at the end of the block and approached the scene of the incident. The front doors of houses on both sides of the street swung open, and Elisha's neighbors poured forth, lining the street much as they had so recently done when word of Mrs. Chancellor's accident had begun to spread. Elisha overheard some gasps and sobs and saw more than a few folks averting their eyes or crossing themselves. Others jostled for a better view.

None were closer to the body than Elisha, but he felt a desire neither to avoid the sight nor to get a closer look. Of most interest to him was the sight of Graham Ripper among the first responders. His part in the story remained incomplete, Elisha told himself. The EMT knelt beside the body, confirming that Christopher was indeed dead, and then covering the body to shield it from the view of the onlookers. Elisha knew it would require quite an effort to remove the utility pole and that the body could not be moved in the meantime. He decided against watching and stepped back inside, leaving Ripper and the others to fulfill their purpose.

Part II

CHAPTER THIRTEEN

The Acts of Elisha

"You will be his witness to all men of
what you have seen and heard.
And now what are you waiting for?"
—Acts 22:15–16a

E lisha rose early the next morning, having committed himself the night before to reopening his bookshop this morning, come what may. Whether or not the decision was a wise one, he couldn't say. On the one hand, it hardly seemed the kind of priority that deserved to take precedence over all others on the first morning after receiving a life-altering revelation from his Creator. But on the other, he longed for a sense of normalcy, and after all, going back to work didn't overtly contradict anything Christopher had told him about his purpose. The Author had, after all, chosen to make him a used book dealer, and so returning to his assigned trade and playing out that part couldn't deviate too far from his intended purpose. Or so he repeatedly reassured himself until he truly began to believe so. Besides, he needed time to sort things out, and the slow pace and quietude of his shop would provide a setting conducive to some necessary soul searching and decision making.

He climbed out of bed with unusual alacrity, strode purposefully toward the bathroom, and twisted the tap. The handle felt cold against his warm skin, but soon, he knew, the water would be running hot and steam would fill the room. The anticipation of stepping beneath it delighted him as it never before had. Elisha found new pleasure in the mundane familiarity of his normal routine, which he had neglected for so long. It felt much, he noted, like the denouement of a story, when the tension the writer had been building was released and the reader could enjoy a deep refreshing breath and the satisfaction of knowing that all had turned out well after all. The tumultuous events of earlier in the week, Elisha imagined, represented the tale's conflict, and his most recent encounter its resolution. So things must surely be drawing to a close, in spite of Christopher's cagey insistence that Elisha still had things to do and that the end remained up in the air. Perhaps Christopher had only been afraid to admit as much for fear of letting the cat out of the bag for some transcendent reason.

After all, Elisha had indeed been proven correct; at least as far as the essentials, and a tidy concluding chapter would wrap up the few remaining loose ends very nicely. Then, what? Not twenty-four hours earlier, the thought that his tale could end at any moment filled him with dread. Mrs. Chancellor's end hadn't been the sort to make one look ahead calmly to his own. On top of that, Unwin's disappearance, in some ways more unsettling even than his neighbor's demise, hardly lived up to the traditional fairy tale ending in which the heroes lived happily ever after. Even Christopher's end had been shocking and bizarre. Yet he had said he intended it to reassure Elisha, and somehow it had. On this new morning, he felt satisfied and untroubled in the face of the very same unknown future that had terrified him just yesterday. Elisha didn't quite understand why, but the counterintuitive fact remained. Christopher had indeed walked toward his fate willingly, not so much bravely as nonchalantly—as if it amounted to nothing, a mere comma partway through a sentence that would continue on the next page. Very likely he had already popped up in some other story, or maybe sat at a desk somewhere farther back and higher up, crafting another new world to inhabit with more new characters. It was a powerful lesson. Beyond death lay reason for hope and a fresh start. As a result, Elisha's fears had dissipated overnight, leaving him filled with a serene readiness to face the future and learn what it had in store for him.

Many of Christopher's words still puzzled him and the overall significance of his visit remained elusive. Some of the answers he'd received from his visitor defied easy analysis, and Christopher had been anything but clear about what would happen next. Still, Elisha contented himself with a wait-and-see approach. So his ambitions for this day extended only so far as reopening his shop and resuming business as usual. He'd spent too much time elsewhere of late, doing other things and thinking other-worldly thoughts. For now, he'd let things take their course. After all, nothing about his world had changed in the least; he simply understood it in a new and more profound way. As far as the future went, he no longer distrusted the Author and felt no further trepidation about leaving his fate in his congenial and capable hands. He vaguely regretted having failed to ask Christopher for the Author's true name, but most likely, he'd only have been assured that he didn't need to know. So that was that.

Elisha turned on his bedside radio and listened to his favorite station's morning show while climbing out of his pajamas and fetching a towel and washcloth from the linen closet. This morning's playlist seemed cheerier than on other mornings, but he attributed that to his imagination—a mere perception resulting from his hopeful new outlook.

He headed for the shower and stepped in. Gradually, the liquid warmth put his stiff muscles and tense tendons at ease. He lathered himself vigorously, giving special attention to his face and neck. He shampooed, rinsed, and repeated, all to the broadcasted rhythm of

Start Me Up. He lingered under the water even after he'd finished cleansing himself, just to savor the feel of the water on his world-weary body. What was the term favored by the romantic writers? *Weltschmerz*, wasn't it? He'd learned about it in school while studying the works of Heinrich Heine, but the Romanticists never even hinted that the effects could be showered away. Maybe they didn't know.

By the time he emerged, dripping but invigorated, the first rays of the rising sun had set the bedroom aglow. To Elisha it seemed like the promise of a bright new day and a welcome fresh start. He fairly bounded to his closet, giving a playful salute to the bedside table lamp as he passed. Selecting a smart outfit that reflected his steadily brightening mood, he dressed, then lingered long enough to make the bed, something he only occasionally bothered with. Then, nearly forgetting to turn off the radio and still humming to himself even after he did so, he trotted lightly down the stairs to fix himself a hearty morning meal before setting out for the shop.

Dirty dishes left from the previous day filled the sink and, less conveniently still, littered the stovetop. One look at the untidy mess dissuaded Elisha from making himself something hot but couldn't darken his mood. He contentedly opted instead for cold cereal, along with the last of the orange juice. He selected a box of Raisin Bran from the pantry, filled a bowl with flakes, and covered them with a dose of milk. Then he reached for the juice that Christopher had placed in the refrigerator the day before, hoping to find enough left to fill a glass. He lifted the carton and shook it. It was full and unopened, as if yesterday's meal had never happened even though the dirty dishes testified that it had. "Very funny," he said out loud to no one in his own world. But then he smiled in spite of himself and added, "Thanks." Pouring himself a glassful, he held it aloft and declared, "Here's to you, Chris."

He ate slowly, pausing between each mouthful to scan yester-day's newspaper, which he found waiting for him even though he didn't remember retrieving it following Christopher's exit. As always, it carried both good news and bad. The local college basketball team remained undefeated, he saw, but on the other hand, he had once again failed to predict the winning Powerball numbers. Well, that wasn't really news, and nothing to grieve over. Tomorrow would be another day. Though maybe not. Not if he fulfilled his purpose before midnight. On this matter too, he'd have to wait and see.

He successfully chased the last of the raisins around the bottom of his bowl with his spoon, gulped down a full glass of fresh juice, then took both the bowl and the glass to the sink, and added them to the growing pile of dishes waiting to be washed. Something to look forward to when he returned home in the evening, he told himself wryly.

He headed toward his front door past a much nicer living room sofa and easy chair than he remembered owning. The sight made him pause, and as he did, his eyes noticed some really first-rate crown molding and walls adorned with art much nicer than he could readily afford. An abstract something-or-other signed by an artist named Wang now graced the dining room wall opposite an unexpected bay window, and a colorful but unfamiliar autumn landscape livened up the surprisingly large living room. Elisha's gaze, though, continued on toward the fireplace, also new, over which hung *Storm on the Sea of Galilee*, by Rembrandt. Elisha's eyes went wide. He didn't know much about art, but he knew what he liked, and he didn't like the idea of a masterpiece stolen from a Boston art museum in 1990 turning up without explanation in his home.

Feeling as though Christopher had really gone too far this time, Elisha hurried across the room, took down the painting, and had a closer look. The image had greatly impressed him ever since the first time he came across it in a coffee table book, and as he held the framed masterpiece to the morning light, it looked a touch too similar to that printed rendition. He turned it over. A sticker affixed to the lower right-hand corner read: "Limited edition print. #101 of 100." Elisha let out a long breath and idly wondered whether he'd ever remember how the gorgeous print had gotten there. He admitted to himself that it looked quite inspirational despite being only a copy and noted to himself that someday he'd have to invite a visitor to ask how he'd acquired it so they could both learn about it at the same time.

For now though, he left the *faux* masterpiece leaning against the hearth and stepped outside. There, he noticed that the clean-up in the street had been completed. Not a trace remained of Christopher's remains. The pole had been replaced and rewired. Normalcy had returned, down to the very smallest detail. Elisha liked it.

"Howdy there, neighbor!" an unfamiliar voice called from over his left shoulder, just as Mrs. Chancellor's had done so often. The voice wasn't hers this time, but in this familiar setting, Elisha wouldn't have felt very surprised if he had turned to find her there, as if nothing had happened, greeting him as she had done so many times before. But the face that his eyes fell upon wasn't hers, either. It wasn't a single face at all, in fact, but a pair of faces, each far younger than the one he had grown accustomed to seeing in Mrs. Chancellor's front yard.

"Good morning," Elisha offered, his voice betraying his puzzlement. "Who are you folks?"

"We're your new neighbors," the young man said. "We just bought this house."

"Oh!" Elisha blurted. "I didn't know it was for sale yet. I mean, only three days ago... Well, things are happening so quickly, that's all."

"Aren't they?" the young woman agreed. "It's all so very fortunate." She held a cane in her hand and her eyes seemed to look straight through Elisha and focus on something or someone unseen standing behind him. Elisha realized that she was blind.

"We've been hoping to find a place in this neighborhood, and the timing couldn't have been better," her husband agreed. "It's like it was meant to be. In truth, we haven't actually signed the papers yet, but we just finished the final walkthrough and everything seems to be in order. We found a charred spot on the floor of the master bedroom, but we're not going to quibble over that. The new carpet will cover it anyway. We hope to move in later today."

Elisha smiled. "Well, welcome to the neighborhood, I guess. I'm Elisha."

"It's good to meet you," said the young man, extending his hand. "My name is Compeyson, and this is my wife, Missy."

Elisha smiled again, coyly this time, as one does in response to an inside joke he's sure no one else in the room understands. "Compeyson," he repeated, shaking the man's hand. "That's a rare name."

"Sure enough," the young man chuckled. "It's from—"

"Dickens," Elisha interrupted. *Great Expectations.* Compeyson was quite the villain, as I recall."

The young man laughed. "That's right. It was my mother's favorite novel. I don't think I've ever before met anyone who made the connection. But I'm not at all like my namesake, I assure you."

"I can see that," Elisha quipped, pointing a thumb in Missy's direction.

"Say," Missy interjected, "we'd love to get to know our new neighbor. Why don't you come round later on and have a cup of coffee? We should be moved in by the end of the day."

"Well, I suppose I could do that," Elisha granted. "I'll be working at my bookshop until five. Could I come by after dinner?"

"That's perfect," Missy acknowledged. "I'll make a dessert and we can get better acquainted. Don't forget!"

Elisha assured her that he wouldn't and silently wondered how Missy's dessert would compare to Mrs. Chancellor's freshly baked cookies. He thanked Compeyson and Missy for the invitation and climbed into the saddle of his bicycle. In just a moment, he was pedaling toward his waiting bookshop.

Elisha couldn't help thinking the unexpected encounter with his new neighbors seemed out of place. Outwardly, they seemed pleasant enough—quite a change from Mrs. Chancellor but all in all not the sort of neighbors to give one cause for concern. He could have done a lot worse. But he couldn't help feeling uneasy once again. Their very presence raised new doubts in his mind about the course his story might be taking. After his rendezvous with Christopher, he'd assumed things were gradually winding down toward an inevitable if still uncertain conclusion. The plot had been clarified. The mysterious unseen benefactor had been revealed, and the entrances and exits of key players explained. Elisha's ultimate purpose remained unfinished, to be sure, but all the necessary pieces were assembled—or so he had thought—and merely awaited the right set of circumstances to bring them all together in the proper setting so the final act could be played out. Why then should the Author introduce two new characters this late in the tale? Compeyson and Missy struck him as two unnecessary and awkward complications—a tangent his story would be better off without.

He'd not shared this thought with them, of course. To anyone lacking his revolutionary worldview, such an observation could only be insulting. And maybe even more so to someone who understood his new perspective. And yet it remained true all the same. Bringing new neighbors into the drama at this point wasn't good style. His tale had already reached a climax. The tension had been resolved. Introducing new neighbors into a story already nearly over made no sense. It represented a new loose end at a time when loose ends were meant to be tied down once and for all.

Elisha wondered what it could mean. Perhaps nothing at all. Just an unfortunate, *faux pas*. Christopher had hinted that the Author could be clumsy at times when crafting his work. Compeyson and Missy could be just two flaws that cropped up unintended. If so, the Author might realize his mistake and edit them out of Elisha's life before his workday ended. If so, he supposed he'd lose all recollection of ever having met them. Because for all intents and purposes, he wouldn't have.

But somehow, Elisha didn't think they'd vanish. They weren't the sort of careless error a sloppy writer might make. Not having the foresight to place a table lamp where it might be needed later in the story made sense in its own way, but consciously inserting two people into the closing pages of a tale with no purpose in mind seemed very unlikely. Everyone had a purpose, Christopher had assured him. So they must be here for a reason, Elisha mused. A purpose. What exactly it could be eluded him. He wondered if they themselves had any inkling or sense of destiny. Probably not. So few people bother to think of such things. But Elisha did.

It was yet another mystery, but he pushed it to the back of his mind as he neared his bookshop, determining to let nothing interfere with his plan to keep regular business hours. But he anticipated an intriguing evening—far more stimulating than simply catching up on his dishwashing—with some interesting conversation over dessert in Mrs. Chancellor's old kitchen.

CHAPTER FOURTEEN

Being and Nothingness

*We also rejoice in our sufferings, because we know that
suffering produces perseverance; perseverance, character;
and character, hope. And hope does not disappoint
us, because God has poured out his love into our
hearts by the Holy Spirit, whom he has given us.*
—Romans 5:3–5

Elisha pedaled the final mile to the shop. His legs began to
ache more than usual, and he was pleased that the final leg
of the trip was entirely downhill. Still, he couldn't attribute
his fatigue entirely to physical exertion. Maybe the old writers hadn't
been so ignorant after all. Maybe it took more than a single hot
shower to beat down *weltschmerz* for more than an hour or two. He
felt it returning, gradually to be sure, yet unmistakably. He feared
he'd need to seek out more unusual diversions than just a routine
workday in order to keep it in check. Maybe a vacation? But he'd
only just returned to work. A new friend? He pondered what sort of
a relationship might develop with his new neighbors, and what he'd
feel comfortable revealing to them about himself. For the present he
planned on being cautious.

He arrived at the shop having encountered not a trace of fog, unlocked the door, loaded his arms with wood from the pile, and ventured inside. The familiar and pleasant smell of old paper filled his nostrils. Soon, he knew, it would mingle with the aroma of burning hickory—a promising start to the day.

He started the fire and flipped the cardboard sign in the window from "Sorry, We're Closed" to "Open," wondering how many customers would venture by on the first day after Christmas. Traditionally, this was a time when readers more typically stayed at home to curl up with books they'd received the day before. Nothing commanded a book lover's attention more unwaveringy than a brand-new title. Well, if it proved to be a slow day, Elisha would have no complaints. He'd have time to take stock. He'd put it to good use. Elisha knew he'd reflect on Christopher's words in every quiet interlude for a good, long time and still never unravel their full significance.

He wandered behind the sales counter and sat down. Only then did he realize he'd left his copy of *Bleak House* at home. At that moment, it still lay on the night table next to his bed, where he'd placed it the night Mrs. Chancellor had remembered her mother for the first time and then forgotten not to go up in flames. Forgetfulness seemed to play a major role in his life's story, he noted. Why had he forgotten Christopher's warning not to follow him out the door? And what might be the consequences, if any? It made him wonder whether he'd forgotten anything else, but he couldn't quite remember.

So he stopped trying and settled in for a long, peaceful day, wondering who might walk through his door over the next eight hours and what they'd be looking for. But as the morning passed, no one did. He got up several times to stoke the fire. He pulled a volume from the shelves to help him pass the time, diligently avoiding Dickens and selecting instead *The Compleat Angler* by Isaak Walton—a safe choice, he assured himself. He wandered back behind the counter, flipped open the cover, and began reading:

You that have heard many grave, serious men pity Anglers; let me tell you, Sir, there be many men that are by others taken to be serious and grave men, whom we contemn and pity. Men that are taken to be grave, because nature hath made them of a sour complexion; money-getting men, men that spend all their time, first in getting, and next, in anxious care to keep it; men that are condemned to be rich, and then always busy or discontented: for these poor rich-men, we Anglers pity them perfectly, and stand in no need to borrow their thoughts to think ourselves so happy.

Elisha couldn't agree more. Life was too short to be all about business. Even before learning the true nature of the world he moved in, he'd never understood the overwhelming drive to acquire, to compete, to advance at the expense of others. Life, he had always prayed, had to be more than a zero-sum game played by winners and losers. He'd been told such ideas were quaint and outdated and escapist. Maybe so. But he preferred old-fashioned values all the same. His aversion to "nature red in tooth and claw" stemmed not from a fear that he'd find himself among the losers, the prey, but rather because he detested the idea of finding himself among the successful predators who came out on top at too great a cost. The Will to Power had no appeal for him. No, bicycles and the pen for me, Elisha mused. He'd leave the internal combustion engine and the sword to others.

He'd never actually been a fisherman, but Walton's words stirred something deep inside him that had always been there, waiting to be aroused, and Elisha began thinking what a pleasure it would be to take a fishing holiday. Not at this time of year certainly, but as soon as the weather turned warmer. Bass season opened in April, he thought.

If his story hadn't reached its conclusion by then, maybe he could get a license and discover for himself what made Walton prefer the life of an angler to the life of rich-men.

Lunchtime came and went, but no customers did. Elisha finished the book and replaced it on the shelf where he'd found it, still excited over applying its lessons up on Lake Tiber in the spring. For now, though, he had a shop to run, so he returned to his place behind the counter and waited. Half an hour later, he had grown itchy yet again and went in search of another book. In "British Classics," the same alcove where he'd selected *The Compleat Angler*, he found *Three Men in a Boat* by Jerome K. Jerome, a writer who never failed to entertain him. He flipped open the cover, turned over the title page, and dived in:

> "What we want is rest," said Harris. "Rest and a complete change," said George. "The overstrain upon our brains has produced a general depression throughout the system. Change of scene, and absence of the necessity for thought, will restore the mental equilibrium."

Within an hour, Elisha had forgotten all about his planned fishing expedition and instead immersed himself in the dream of flying to England and taking a slow boat ride down the Thames. No one came to mind with whom he could share the adventure, to say nothing of a dog, but he could make do on his own, he convinced himself.

Evening drew near before at last the shop door opened, and a young woman stepped through. At first she took no notice of Elisha sitting amid the shelves and counters and books as she took in her surroundings—so well did he blend in with the background. He, on the other hand, was far away, floating on the Thames, and hadn't noticed her come in. When she caught sight of him silently perusing his book, she announced her presence by saying, "Good afternoon. What a warm and cozy place this is on such a chilly day. And what a wonderful selection of books you have. I feel sure I'll be able to find what I need here."

Elisha received this sort of polite introduction all the time, but hearing his shop praised never ceased to please him. "Thank you," he replied quite sincerely. "May I help you find something particular, or would you just like to browse?"

"Do you have any books on philosophy?" the customer asked. "I've been studying the existentialists. I've only just finished *Being and Nothingness*, and I enjoyed it so much that I'm looking for more of the same."

"Alcove six," Elisha offered. "I believe you might find a few first editions among the stacks, if you are interested in that sort of thing, and if you can read French, of course. Otherwise, there is lots to choose from. I don't get many people asking for Sartre and that crowd, so when I get a new title, it tends to stay on the shelf for a while."

"Oh thank you! As a matter of fact, I spent a semester abroad in Paris and am well acquainted with the language. A first edition of *Nothingness* would be a wonderful find. I've only read it in translation."

"Good luck," Elisha called after her as she ducked beneath a low wooden beam and through an archway in search of alcove six. He watched her until she receded out of sight, then turned his attention once more to his book. More minutes passed, and before long, he was fully absorbed. The young philosophy student, likewise fully engaged in her quest, made hardly a sound, and soon faded entirely from Elisha's mind. Nearly an hour passed before she returned, several volumes beneath her arm.

Elisha looked up from his reading, mildly surprised to remember that he had not been alone in the shop, and hoping he had not been singing to himself as he sometimes did when he knew no one could hear. "It looks like you found what you came for," he observed.

"Yes, more than I had hoped for. You were right about *Nothingness*. I found a first edition with the dust jacket in wonderful condition. It looks like it's never been read. Can you imagine? But it's my gain, I guess. And these other titles are a treasure too. I'll take them all. They should more than satisfy my curiosity for now. Thank you!" She handed her selections to Elisha.

"You're very welcome," Elisha said, and then added, "Nothing pleases me more than helping someone who loves good books." Even as he said it, he wondered whether maybe it might be tied to his purpose. Could it be as simple as that? Selling books to readers who loved them? Probably not. He'd been doing as much for years. If that was his purpose, the story should have ended before it had even begun.

"Well," the young student admitted, "you've done your job very well, then. I couldn't be happier. It's like a second Christmas!"

"You must really enjoy the existentialists," Elisha observed, wondering why, but to each his own, he decided.

"Oh I do," the student gushed. "Have you read them yourself?"

"No, not in any depth at least," Elisha confessed.

"You absolutely must give them a try."

"Someday, maybe. For the most part, I prefer Victorian novels. I find that a good novelist can unlock truth and present it in a way that essayists and philosophers struggle to explain."

"Yes, sometimes, I suppose, but books like these have taught me to understand the world in a whole new light. So much of what we see all around us is just an illusion—a made-up reality, if only we all had the insight to see it."

The observation intrigued Elisha, coming close as it did to hitting the mark. He wondered whether maybe he had, in fact, misjudged the existentialists. "Oh, and you simply must read *Nothingness* in particular," she continued. "The author speaks to me so clearly. He introduced me to a whole new way of understanding things—things I'd never suspected before."

Elisha felt a rush of excitement.

"The Author?" he asked expectantly. "You've met the Author?"

The young student giggled. "Well, no, don't be silly. Sartre's been dead for more than thirty years, and I'm only twenty-one. But his writing still speaks to me. Until I read *Nothingness*, I felt like I was a victim of circumstances, that my life didn't matter—that I had no freedom to chart my own course and that life amounted to a meaningless quest for meaningless goals in a meaningless universe."

It sounded all too familiar to Elisha. "I suppose a great many people feel that way. But now you've found your purpose?"

"No. I've found that I need to overcome my sense of nothingness by creating my own purpose. Because the universe really *is* meaningless, apart from whatever rationality I'm able to impose upon it. Purpose is all just part of the illusion, but at least, I can take control of the illusion."

Elisha decided that the two of them stood miles apart, after all, even though only the sales counter separated them. "I've been thinking a lot about my own purpose lately," he said.

"Well, I don't believe any of us have one overarching purpose, just lots of little purposes that crop up along the road of life—things like finding a really well-stocked bookshop, for example, and making a satisfying purchase. But I don't think destiny or fate enters into it. I just decided I wanted some good books, so I exercised my own free will and found some. But that's the end of it. Job's done. Now it's on to my next stop."

"Well, I hope not," Elisha admitted. "It seems to me there must be a master plan. At least that's what I've been led to believe by someone who ought to know. As for free will, that's another question.

I've been told by a well-informed friend that I have a say in my own destiny, but only within finite boundaries."

"Well, don't believe everything you hear," the student advised, trying to be helpful. "Some people know nothing, despite what they say."

Elisha thought it an ironic thing for a devoted disciple of Sartre to conclude, but didn't say so.

"If I were you, I wouldn't put too much faith in grand purposes," the student advised. "Think about it: How many times in your life have you dreamed big dreams—a new car, a new job, a new relationship—and it's all you can think about and you just know that if only you could have it everything would fall into place and your troubles would be over and you'd live happily ever after. How many times has reality lived up to your expectations? Has it ever? I promise you, if you ever get that new car, you'll find that your best friend just bought a bigger, more expensive model, and you'll be dissatisfied. When you land the great new job, you'll find that the new boss is a jerk, and you can't stand being around him. And the new relationship that you placed so much hope in turns out to be a one-night stand who wasn't half as serious about you as you were about her. Trust me, don't get your hopes up. The only good that comes from fulfilling your dreams is that the illusion is shattered. You realize that they amounted to nothing all along, and once you see that, you can get on with your life."

Elisha had to admit that that's how things played out, as often as not. But the young student's explanation wasn't the only one that might account for it. "Couldn't it just be that all those things let us down because they were never meant to be the objects of our quest? Maybe the lesson we're meant to learn isn't that quests are futile and that there's no meaning to life, but only that we're looking for it in the wrong place?"

The friendly young student smiled. "That's a pleasant thought, but believe me, I've looked everywhere. There's no lasting satisfaction, and no purpose. There's just nothingness."

It sounded to Elisha like the end of the conversation, so he said, "I hope you like the books, because there's no refund if they let you down."

The gentle ribbing went over the student's head. "Oh, I've no fear of that! I'm sure they will be absolutely fulfilling. Sartre never fails to satisfy me. Thanks again!" She turned and retreated through the door without noticing Elisha shaking his head and chuckling to himself.

CHAPTER FIFTEEN

Immanent and Transcendent

*Then Philip ran up to the chariot and heard
the man reading Isaiah the prophet. "Do you
understand what you are reading?" Philip asked.
"How can I," he said, "unless someone explains it to me?"
So he invited Philip to come up and sit with him.*
—*Acts 8:30–31*

Elisha prepared himself a quick, microwaveable dinner, hastily wolfed it down, then tossed his empty plate on top of the pile in his sink, which he decided he'd put off washing until after his visit next door. Heading into the living room, he bundled up for the dash across his front yard to Compeyson and Missy's front door. It struck him as a nuisance to have to put on multiple layers for such a short trip, but the night had grown bitterly cold and all things considered, it was time well spent.

Bracing himself, he flung open the door, burst through, and hastened toward the front porch light beckoning him from not more than thirty yards away—the one Mrs. Chancellor had never used, but which now glowed cheerily in defiance of the bitter night. Elisha reached the door, rang the bell, and waited for the door to swing open. It didn't. Elisha shivered in spite of himself. The porch light bathed the front stoop in a yellowish, warm, picture-postcard hue, Elisha noted, but provided no actual protection against the sub-freezing evening air. He rang again. He could no longer feel his nose. He idly wondered if perhaps, like Unwin, it had disappeared. Then he sneezed loudly and sniffled involuntarily, as if to confirm that his proboscis remained in place and fully functional. At last he heard footsteps from inside and the sound of a deadbolt lock being unlatched. The door opened and Missy stood silhouetted against the brightly lit living room behind her. Elisha couldn't help thinking that the outline of her body formed a pleasant shape and felt half ashamed for having noticed it, even though she couldn't realize that he was staring. He remembered, at least, to announce himself. "Hello, Missy. It's Elisha, your neighbor."

"Elisha! Come on in," Missy said, stepping aside so he could comply. "I'm so sorry to have kept you waiting outside. I'm not yet accustomed to getting around in the new house so I'm a bit slow. It wouldn't do to make a wrong turn and go tumbling down the stairs, would it?"

"I certainly wouldn't want to be responsible for that," Elisha answered light-heartedly. "No apology necessary."

"I was doing some tidying up in the master bedroom. There's a funny acrid smell in there and I thought wiping everything down might make it less noticeable. It really needs a good airing out, but that might have to wait until spring. I'm not about to open any windows until things warm up quite a bit."

"I don't blame you," Elisha agreed, closing the front door behind himself as he stepped through into the warm interior.

"Did the previous owner smoke?" Missy asked.

"No," Elisha answered truthfully, "except maybe a little bit at the very end."

"Well, that's all right. I just wouldn't want you to think I'd burned something in the kitchen. By the way, most of my pots and dishes are still in boxes, so I couldn't get very fancy with the dessert I promised you. I've just made us all some cookies to go with our coffee. I hope that's all right."

"Quite all right," Elisha assured his host. "In fact, it's kind of a tradition. Mrs. Chancellor, the woman who used to live here, invited me in for cookies just last week. It was the last time we spoke. She... left unexpectedly," Elisha explained without really explaining. But other than her smoking habits, Missy didn't seem interested in the house's previous occupant or her personal business and didn't pursue the matter.

"Here, let me take your coat and hat," she offered. "I'll just lay them on the sofa for you, if that's all right. The foyer closet is stacked with boxes, and we didn't get to the hangers yet. But now let's head into the kitchen. There's less clutter in there and room to sit down and relax. I don't know about you, but it's been a busy day around here and it will feel good to get off my feet."

She led the way—an unnecessary courtesy since Mrs. Chancellor's home was identical in layout to Elisha's own, though a mirror image. In the kitchen, they found Compeyson already seated, reading a newspaper and dunking a cookie into a hot mug of coffee. The smell reminded Elisha of the last time he'd been in the room. Little enough had changed, although Elisha suspected it wouldn't be long before Missy introduced her own personal touches into the space, unintentionally eradicating the last vestiges Mrs. Chancellor's existence.

"Good evening, Elisha," Compeyson mumbled through a mouthful of oatmeal and raisins. "Pardon me for not waiting. I've worked up a good appetite today, and there's nothing like a hot cup of coffee after a full day's labor, don't you think? Sit and help yourself. Missy, bring the coffee pot for our guest."

Elisha sat and selected a cookie from a heaping pile on a paper plate in the center of the round kitchen table. It felt warm and soft to the touch. He took a bite. It tasted good, but didn't compare to Mrs. Chancellor's. A bit too much sugar, he thought to himself, but he said, "Mmm, this really hits the spot, thank you." Missy placed the coffee pot and a mug in front of him and he poured himself a drink.

"So, Elisha," Compeyson began, "tell us about yourself. How long have you lived in this neighborhood? What's it like?" Elisha noted that the questions pointed in two entirely different directions and wondered which way to go. He felt less comfortable talking about himself and more inclined to shift the focus elsewhere.

Already, he decided, this evening shared more in common with his last visit to this room than just the smell of freshly baked cookies. Elisha thought back to his little experiment, when he had encouraged Mrs. Chancellor to ask him about learning to ride a bike, and to the feeling he had when she complied—that pause before the memory had coalesced, when his mind was still a blank slate waiting to be written on. Now he felt it happening again. Compeyson had asked how long he had lived at his current address, and Elisha realized that he didn't know. On the one hand "forever" certainly seemed like the correct response, because he had no explicit recollection of ever moving in. It wasn't yet part of his story. It lay among those unnecessary tidbits that had been left out. His story had begun in his current home, and everything before that was without form and void. But already the question had been asked, the trigger pulled, and Elisha sensed a realignment occurring inside his head.

"I've lived here for twenty-eight years," he heard himself say, and memories of moving in took up residence in his mind. Henceforth he'd be able to answer any questions about the event that might follow. He knew Compeyson and Missy would attribute his awkward pause before answering the simple question to nothing more than the need to do some hasty arithmetic in his head. He saw no good reason to clarify things. Still, he chose to steer the conversation away from himself and toward talk about the neighborhood.

"Trash day is Thursday," Elisha advised, "except when there's a holiday earlier in the week. Then it gets pushed back a day to Friday. The mail gets delivered every day at just about two o'clock. A little earlier on Saturday. And if you need to borrow a hedge trimmer or a post hole digger, Mr. Fabrio at number 349 is the one to ask. He's a kind-hearted soul who enjoys yard work but doesn't like loaning out his tools, so if you ask to use one, he'll offer to do the job for you himself."

Compeyson chuckled. "Good to know," he acknowledged.

Missy said nothing. Elisha got the feeling that, having answered the door and invited him inside, she intended to speak as infrequently as possible. Her husband, Elisha sensed, was the more outgoing of the two.

"So how about you folks?" Elisha asked, shifting the focus of their conversation back onto his hosts. "You said this morning that you've been hoping to settle in the area. Where are you from originally, and what brings you here?"

Compeyson took a deep breath that bordered on a sigh. "Well," he began hesitantly, after casting a furtive glance at Missy. "We're from, well, out of state, but I can't really say for sure what drew us to this locale. It's almost like it's fate—except that I don't believe in fate, so it can't be that. But whatever it was, it was irresistible. Not long ago, Missy began feeling the strongest compulsion to sell our home and move here. She kept it to herself at first, thinking I'd just laugh at her or worse if she mentioned it. But then one morning over breakfast, she just couldn't contain herself any longer, and out of the blue, she burst out that she'd been thinking of moving." Elisha glanced at Missy and saw that she was blushing. "I asked her what had gotten her thinking this way, and she turned red and said she really didn't know because she had always felt perfectly happy right where we were, but that she had grown so obsessed lately with the compulsion to move that she had trouble sleeping at night.

"Well, once it was all out in the open something had to be done about it. You might think I'd have been upset. Certainly Missy had feared that I'd be. But, Elisha, let me tell you something." He paused and Elisha could almost hear the gears turning inside Compeyson's head as he contemplated the right words to use. But instead of telling Elisha anything, he asked a question. "Are you married, Elisha?"

"Never."

"I thought not," Compeyson replied without explanation. "So you probably don't have much experience with women's intuition." Elisha conceded as much. "Well," Compeyson continued, "I used to believe that sort of talk was just nonsense, but Missy's got it in spades. I mean, it's probably not even right to call it that. She has these, well, hunches I guess, or premonitions, or whatever. And I've learned not to ignore them. So when she blurted out that she thought we ought to move, I didn't question it, hard as that might be for you to imagine. We agreed to wrap up our former lives and begin afresh in a new place. The oddest thing was that we both felt drawn to here, of all places. Not New York, or Chicago, or Florida, or Hawaii, but here. We couldn't put our finger on any special reason, but every time we thought maybe we'd check out the possibilities in some other direction, she'd start getting headaches and dizzy spells that just wouldn't go away. The only thing that made her feel like her old self was having me read her the local real estate listings. So while we don't quite understand how or why, we knew that this must be the place for us. Like I said, it can only be fate—except of course that it can't be that."

Elisha marveled that these near-strangers—or one of them, anyway—felt willing to share such an uncanny story with him. Compeyson's account made perfect sense to Elisha, of course. Missy felt compelled to move here because the Author had compelled her, for reasons of his own. It was as simple as that. But it must appear altogether inexplicable to his neighbors apart from the workings of fate, which Compeyson had excluded at the outset as a plausible explanation. Elisha doubted now that he'd leave their new home with a solution to the question he'd hoped to have answered. "How interesting," he replied, hiding all these thoughts behind an attitude of nonchalance. "Well, rest assured that this is a nice place to put down roots—in my humble opinion anyway. I'm sure you'll feel right at home here in no time. In fact, I'll bet that by the time you're fully unpacked, you'll be quite glad you paid attention to Missy's little nudges."

"Oh, I'm sure we will. In fact, we feel very comfortable here already. It's like we were shaped perfectly to fit in here. We don't regret our move at all. It's just that, well, we were kind of hoping that maybe one of our new neighbors might have some sort of explanation for the strange things Missy's been feeling. We thought maybe you might be able to make some sense of it all and let us in on why we seem to have been irresistibly drawn here at this particular time."

Elisha wondered at the Author's purposes as well, but as yet he had no better idea than Compeyson. Ironically, his neighbor's most urgent question was the same as his own. Elisha had come hoping they would tell him why they were here, and they had invited him hoping he'd tell them. But neither had a clue. What purpose did these people serve? Elisha remained convinced that they held the answer, whether or not they yet realized it.

"What makes you imagine that I would know why you feel drawn to our little town?" he wondered aloud.

"No reason in particular," Compeyson admitted. "We just thought maybe everyone who comes here to live feels the same things we've been feeling, and that it's a well-known phenomenon that you've all discussed among yourselves and can now explain."

"It's not," Elisha declared apologetically. "I've never heard anything resembling your story from anyone around here. Of course I haven't really polled the neighbors to ask why they moved here, so I can't say for sure that no one else has ever shared your experience, but if so, they've kept it to themselves."

Compeyson and especially Missy looked deflated. They'd clearly had high hopes for this evening's conversation that Elisha had just dashed. "So you have no idea what to make of all this?"

"Hmmm," Elisha said, hoping he sounded thoughtful. "I'm not sure I can help you in that regard, but then again it's just possible. Would you mind if I ask you one or two personal questions? Your answers might call something to mind." Missy looked somewhat uncomfortable with this, but Compeyson unhesitatingly gave Elisha permission. "Pardon me, but I'm curious about your name, Compeyson. You said this morning your mother was inspired by *Great Expectations*. Have you ever read the book?"

"Heavens, no," Compeyson answered with a sour expression on his face. "I can't imagine anything less profitable! I've never enjoyed reading, and if I were ever to start for some entirely unforeseen reason, I'd hardly begin with Dickens. The thought of investing my time in such a manner holds no attraction for me. Why? What does my name have to do with anything?"

"Probably nothing," Elisha assured him. "I'm just wondering if there are any clues to the meaning of your unusual story hidden somewhere in your childhood memories. I'm no psychologist, but I thought maybe if you told me more about your upbringing it might explain your compulsion to move." Elisha felt guilty about misleading his host.

Truthfully, whatever circumstances might have conspired to bring Compeyson and Missy into Elisha's story didn't especially interest him. The answer to why they were here was beyond dispute. The Author had brought them. What nagged at Elisha's imagination was not their motivation for moving, but rather the Author's reasons for moving them. He took it as a given that his new neighbors' reasons for coming and the Author's reasons for bringing them here would be entirely different, and that the first was trivial—a mere literary device needed to move the story along but which could easily have been different if the Author had been in a different mood. Only the second question really interested him. The first, as Christopher would say, was immanent. The transcendent reason mattered more. In fact, Elisha sensed it was pivotal.

CHAPTER SIXTEEN

Déjà Vu All Over Again

*"I know your deeds; you have a reputation of being
alive, but you are dead. Wake up! Strengthen what
remains and is about to die, for I have not found
your deeds complete in the sight of my God."*
—Revelation 3:1b–2

E lisha hadn't expected his question about the name Compeyson's mother had chosen for him to answer the transcendent question directly. He hoped instead to assess his new neighbor's memories, including whether or not he recalled his mother any more clearly than Mrs. Chancellor had remembered hers. In his estimation, memories provided the key to the puzzle. The Author, Elisha knew, left out everything nonessential to his story. Mrs. Chancellor's mother had been nonessential, so she had no memory of her, at least until it *had* become essential. How he had learned to ride a bicycle had also been unnecessary, so the Author had left that untold as well, until Elisha and Mrs. Chancellor had forced his hand. In contrast, Elisha's bookshop had provided the setting for a key episode in his story—maybe for two—in which important information had come to light, so Elisha needed an intimate familiarity with its every nook and corner. And sure enough, he had it.

Similarly, he calculated, by assessing what details about their own pasts Compeyson and his wife most vividly remembered and which they did not, he could determine what made them important to the story by a painstaking process of elimination. The gaps he needn't consider any further. They'd be dead-ends, unimportant details the Author had omitted because they weren't an essential part of their immanent purpose nor, therefore, his transcendent one. But every crystal-clear memory, potentially at least, held a clue to the essential role the Author had carved out for them—and in turn, how Elisha ought to respond to them. Elisha could only assume that the Author meant for him to react to their presence in a particular way, and that his story would not reach a resolution until he did.

"How about you, Missy?" Elisha prodded. "Is there a story behind your name? Is it short for Melissa? Is it a family name? Maybe a grandmother or a great aunt?"

Missy blushed. "No, it's not a family name. Not exactly anyway. I'm named after my mother's cat, Miss Schrödinger."

Elisha regretted asking and felt his face grow warm, indicating that he was blushing as well. He hadn't meant to embarrass his host, but he clearly had. "Oh. Well, like I said, it probably doesn't have anything to do with anything. You know, maybe this whole thing does just come down to fate after all. Compeyson, you're the second person I've met today who insists that there's no such thing as fate, but who knows? Missy, you didn't know the previous owner of this place, Mrs. Chancellor, but she loved to bake cookies. Now she's gone and I'll never get to enjoy another of her treats. Maybe fate brought you here so you could bless the neighborhood with your baking, just like Mrs. Chancellor used to do. If that's the case, I for one would be perfectly satisfied. You'll be a very welcome addition to our little community, and to my world."

With that, Elisha smacked his lips and helped himself to another oatmeal cookie from the top of the stack at the center of the table. Missy smiled self-consciously, and Elisha congratulated himself for the skill with which he had seemingly changed the subject without really doing so. "Do you have any special hobbies or interests, Compeyson? How do you wind down at the end of the day?"

"I don't have much time for hobbies," Compeyson replied. "I never saw the sense in them. My work comes first. I'm an investment banker, or at least I was. I'm between jobs right now. That's another odd aspect of all this. We moved here without even considering the local job market, so right now I'm unemployed. But not for long. That's just not me. I need to keep myself busy, so as soon as we're settled, I intend to go job hunting. I was reading the 'Help Wanted' section of the paper when you came in. I'm sure there must be several banks in the neighborhood. I'll make the rounds until I find one that's hiring. I'll feel like half a man until I'm bringing home a paycheck again."

At that moment, Compeyson struck Elisha as grave and serious, but that was no reason to be unhelpful. "I pass a bank every day on my way to work," Elisha suggested. "You might check and see what opportunities they have available. It would be convenient, that's for sure. It's just a few miles from here." He scribbled the address on a napkin and pushed it across the table toward Compeyson.

"Thanks, Elisha. I'll look into it. I'll drive Missy crazy inside a week if I'm wandering around the house here with nothing to keep me busy. I love making money and helping others invest theirs. I pity folks who don't have enough drive to turn a nice profit, but when I help them plan for their retirement or invest in the right growth funds, well, there's nothing more satisfying than that. It makes me feel useful, like I have a purpose in life. Hey, maybe I can take a look at your portfolio sometime, Elisha. I might be able to recommend a thing or two."

"I'll keep that in mind," Elisha said cautiously. He envied Compeyson's clear sense of direction, even if it was grave and serious and gave one a sour complexion. It just wasn't for him. "Well, it's getting late, and I've got a sink full of dishes waiting to be washed. I think I'd better be getting back home. But I want to thank you again for inviting me over to get acquainted. I'll give some more thought to your story and if anything occurs to me, I'll let you know. Don't forget to drop by the bank, Compeyson. Thank you for your warm hospitality, Missy." She escorted Elisha to the door and helped him with his coat while Compeyson finished his dessert.

"Thank you for dropping by, Elisha. Did you really like my cookies?"

"Very much," Elisha assured her. Then, because she couldn't know that he was smiling, he took her hand and gave it a gentle squeeze. As she had already done several times throughout the evening, Missy blushed once again.

Elisha stepped back outside and heard the door close behind him. Despite the cold, he paused for a moment on the front step, replaying in his mind the events of the past hour. Then his nose disappeared again, or felt as though it had, and he decided he'd best get himself back home and ponder things in more familiar, warmer surroundings.

The frozen grass crumpled beneath his feet as he scurried, shoulders hunched against the cold, between the houses and through his front door. The evening was still young but like Compeyson, he felt no desire to spend it in a good book, even though quite unlike Compeyson he loved to read. But tonight, he had some thinking of his own to do. He considered warming his chilled bones by lying down on his bed and doing his soul searching from beneath his quilt, but decided against getting too comfortable for fear of dozing off too quickly. Instead, he headed for the kitchen table. Some more coffee would warm him well enough and maybe resharpen his dulled wits.

He walked past the fireplace, where *Storm on the Sea of Galilee* hung just above eye level, and entered the kitchen, making a beeline for the coffee. The pile of dishes waited accusatorily in the sink, but he ignored it for now, giving his full attention to brewing a fresh pot.

"Compeyson," he said aloud, as if to help himself evaluate the significance of his neighbor's unusual name and ponder whether it might hold a clue to his true purpose. He'd already been wondering about Graham Ripper's ironically suggestive moniker. Could Compeyson's, too, reflect some hidden purpose? He quickly decided it didn't—it was just another example of the Author's tendency to borrow from existing works of literature when he needed ideas for his story, Elisha felt sure. It followed the Author's familiar pattern of using Dickens as his inspiration. Every character needs a name, Elisha reasoned, and the Author had simply recycled an exotic and memorable one from a handy source. There seemed no reason to attribute any other significance to it. Compeyson's mother had needed a name for her son, and the Author had needed a name for his character, and this was the one they both gave him, end of story.

And Missy? Two possibilities came to mind. The first followed on the heels of Elisha's previous train of thought. In *Great Expectations,* Compeyson had jilted Miss Havisham, leaving her a spinster for the rest of her life. It might tickle the Author's sense of humor to introduce a married couple into his story whose names approximated those of Dickens' never-to-be bride and groom. If so, then once again Elisha had no good reason to attach any deeper meaning to it all. It meant nothing more than a subtle jest, or the Author's way of correcting a sad injustice by finally bringing the two characters together in marriage—in a sense at least.

But another possibility remained. Missy herself said her name had no connection to Dickens, but rather to a cat. A cat named, in turn, after a renowned physicist who'd wrestled with the nature of reality, just as Elisha had been doing this past week, as well as the young philosophy student who had visited his bookstore. Elisha could almost sense a recurring pattern, as if he was being presented with various takes on the nature of reality—Huxley's, Christopher's, Jean Paul Sartre's, and now Erwin Schrödinger's. What's more, Missy had contributed practically nothing of any real substance to the evening's conversation between her initial welcome and charming farewell. Compeyson had done all the talking—except when Missy shared this one lone thought, almost as if the entire conversation had been prearranged in order to focus Elisha's attention on it. He suspected he had stumbled onto something significant, but if so he couldn't begin to imagine what the Author meant for him to do with it. He'd need to follow this trail much farther in order to discern where it pointed him.

He wished now that he'd not spent all of his time reading fiction but had instead devoted some attention to the physical sciences. It occurred to him that he knew more about fictional characters who'd never really lived than about historical figures who had impacted the world in tangible ways. He tried his best to recall the little he knew about Schrödinger and his famous paradox involving a cat and its possible fates. Did the cat have a name? he wondered at first, then decided it didn't matter. He shook his head to clear it of extraneous, silly thoughts.

Schrödinger, he remembered, had formulated a famous thought experiment to demonstrate that according to one theory of quantum mechanics, a cat confined out of sight in a box could be both dead and alive at the same time. In fact, the theory predicted that the cat *would* be both dead and alive at the same time—until an outside observer intervened. Then, in order to avoid a nonsensical contradiction, one outcome would necessarily give way to the other because, well, because you just can't go around being dead and alive at the same time. That just wouldn't do.

Elisha didn't doubt for a moment that his understanding of the paradox had lots of gaps in it, but essentially, that's what Schrödinger had imagined. Two contradictory outcomes, each equally probable, both awaiting the intervention of a rational observer to see which would give way and which would prevail. Elisha seemed to recall that yet another version of the theory postulated that both outcomes prevailed, and that the moment an observer peeked inside the box to see how the cat was doing, the universe split into two separate realities—one in which the cat lived and another in which he didn't. We'd only get to see one of the outcomes, because we aren't privileged to see into the alternate universe. But Elisha assumed he misunderstood the notion, because he'd been told many times that science excludes the possibility of unseen worlds that exist beyond our ability to detect, measure, and compartmentalize.

Elisha sighed. He didn't know whether he was on to something, or if this was just another extraneous, silly idea. Could there really be a connection between his charmingly attractive new neighbor, her mother's cat, a theoretical physicist, and his own story, which still seemed unfinished but now in a new way? Did the Author mean for him to understand that sooner or later he'd have to look inside a closed system—his own life, Elisha guessed—and by doing so, reduce all possible outcomes to a single destiny? Maybe, but then again, Schrödinger had used his illustration not to depict the way he believed things really were, but instead to demonstrate the absurdity—the sheer improbability—of the existing theories. So maybe that was the Author's intended meaning—that Elisha was heading in the wrong direction entirely and needed to take a different approach if he ever hoped to arrive at truth. Or then again, it could mean nothing at all and for some unfathomable reason Missy's mother just thought "Miss Schrödinger" sounded like a good name for a cat. Elisha idly wondered what name Pavlov had given to his dog. "Montmorency," he wouldn't be surprised to learn.

He shook his head clear once again. Could he have missed some other vital clue hidden among the evening's casual give and take? Elisha searched his memory. Compeyson despised reading, he had said. Elisha couldn't imagine such a thing, but neither did it seem to hold any great potential as a clue. On the contrary, it represented a closed door. The Author clearly favored literary references as a means of communicating subtle ideas to Elisha, but insights Compeyson might otherwise have gained from good authors and passed on to Elisha via fascinating hours of intellectual conversation were eliminated as a means of further revelation by nature of his neighbor's grave aversion to books.

Compeyson also avoided hobbies—another closed door. He was an out-of-work banker who liked making money. That struck Elisha as unremarkable. Who didn't like making money? It was the absolute passion of nearly everyone Elisha knew. It occupied their every waking hour and filled their dreams at night. Money was their first and only true love. It was their God. But it was old news and hardly the sort of thing the Author would use to get Elisha's attention.

What's more, it didn't comport with what Elisha already knew about himself—a preference for bicycles over automobiles, for wood stoves over electric forced-air heaters, for quaint bookshops over banks. If anything, the Author had blessed Elisha with an ambivalence toward money, rather than an attraction. Given their divergent temperaments, Elisha and Compeyson seemed unlikely to become kindred spirits. So what did that leave? Just cats and improbable theories.

Elisha sighed, blew into his coffee, and took a careful sip. It had long since gone cold. He briefly considered drinking it anyway, then thought better of it and emptied it into the sink before turning and heading back through the living room and up the stairs, telling himself the dishes would still be there in the morning. In his bedroom, he took the quilt from its stand and spread it out over top of the bed. He'd need an extra layer tonight. He brushed his teeth, changed into his pajamas, then returned to the bed and sat down once more.

He ran his fingers across the quilt, appreciating its familiarity in the midst of all that seemed so strange of late.

He remembered appreciating his familiar quilt on the morning when all this had started—when he'd overslept by twelve hours. It struck him then that the events of the past day, which he'd been reviewing in his head, all seemed familiar—not exactly like déjà vu, and certainly not in reverse, but familiar nevertheless. More like a rerun than like déjà vu. Had he lived it before? How could that be? He pondered the question. And then he understood. He *had* lived this day once before. Not literally, to be sure, but exactly one week earlier, he had gone to his bookshop, spent some time reading, met with a single customer, then cycled back home and visited with his neighbor—all just as he had once again on this day. And following a rather remarkable conversation he'd returned home to ponder the significance of all that had happened.

A rerun! Elisha felt a shiver of excitement. Could that be it? Could that be why Compeyson and Missy had appeared in his story? Yes, most certainly it could—in fact, it had to be! He was being given a second chance to do something he'd neglected the first time around or had gotten wrong. And then a terrible truth filled Elisha's troubled mind. If this was indeed a rerun, he knew what must happen next. He knew. He knew he'd been wrong when he'd imagined that the Author had playfully brought Compeyson and Miss Havisham together at last. Yes, he'd brought them together, but no, it wouldn't last. In fact, their time together was very nearly at an end.

A week ago, he'd gone to sleep and woke to find his neighbor gone, killed in exactly the same manner as the Lord Chancellor in *Bleak House*. Tomorrow, beyond all doubt, he'd wake to find that Compeyson, just like his literary namesake, had left Missy for good. She would need Elisha's consolation, but his best efforts, he knew, would be futile. She'd be wrecked for life.

CHAPTER SEVENTEEN

Lost and Found

Blessed are those who mourn,
for they will be comforted.
—Matthew 5:4

Elisha woke but dared not open his eyes just yet. Instead, he listened. The previous week, strange sounds coming from outside the house had heralded an unusual and eventful day. This morning he heard nothing. He found the silence encouraging.

Cautiously, he opened one eye. Cold white light flooded the bedroom, but it shared the space with intermittent flashes of blue and red. Elisha's heart sank. Slowly but deliberately, he crawled out of bed, and wrapping himself inside his robe, he stumbled to the window and looked out, correctly anticipating what he'd see.

A police cruiser sat parked in Missy's driveway. Even as Elisha watched, the rooftop light bar, which had been the cause of the light show in his bedroom, went dark, and the cruiser backed out of the driveway and rolled off at an unhurried speed. Elisha took it as his cue to venture next door to console his solitary neighbor.

But he needn't rush. Missy had all the time in the world—a whole lifetime. First, Elisha would get himself together and get a bite to eat. He just might manage to find his way in to his bookshop for at least a part of the morning, although that seemed unlikely, especially if he was rerunning the events of the previous week. Still, he'd best fill his belly so he'd be prepared for whatever turn the day might take.

He stepped into the shower and realized that he had spent a good portion of his time there recently. He could do worse, he decided. The hot water felt good against his back. He thrust his head beneath the showerhead and enjoyed the warmth tickling down the length of his body for several minutes without bothering to lather up. He sighed. For as long as he could remember, he'd never felt fully satisfied by even the longest of showers. They could wash the grime away, but never really soothed his aching muscles and relaxed his nerves. Showers always left him feeling like he needed a bath. Baths, on the other hand, left him more fully refreshed, but feeling sticky, as though he needed a shower. The worst of both worlds, he told himself.

He emerged, dried himself, and got dressed, choosing some casual jeans and a flannel shirt. Downstairs, he poured himself a tall glass of fresh orange juice, forgetting this time to offer thanks, and fixed another bowl of cold cereal. Afterwards he took the dishes to the sink, noting with some annoyance that the ever-growing pile already there had not been washed and put away. Apparently Christopher's friendly little blessings didn't extend to doing the kitchen chores. But it couldn't hurt to wait just another twenty-four hours or so, just to be sure.

And then he could delay no more. He had a job to do and it needed to be done, fruitless as it must surely be. He fetched his overcoat from the closet and retraced his trail from the previous evening, across the space between his house and Missy's, bringing him again to his neighbor's front door. The temperature, he noted, had risen during the night and his nose survived the trek without disappearing. He knocked.

This time the door swung open almost immediately. Apparently Missy had not been unpacking, as she had the night before. "Good morning, Missy," he said, feeling foolish as he did.

"Oh, Elisha!" she exclaimed with dismay upon hearing her new friend's voice. "I'm so glad you're here. I need someone to talk to. Something terrible has happened. Please come in." As she spoke the words, she took Elisha by the arm and pulled him into her living room without waiting for him to reply.

"I saw a police car out front earlier," Elisha said to explain his uninvited arrival. "I hope there's not been any trouble," he added, knowing without being told that there had.

"I really don't know," Missy sobbed through piteous tears. "I can't explain it, but Compeyson is gone. He left without a word sometime during the night. I woke this morning to find an empty house. No explanation, nothing. I'm afraid he won't come back." She began crying out loud without restraint, having trouble making herself understood between her breathless gasps. Elisha felt like a hug would be just the thing for her and wanted to offer one, but at the same time judged that hugging another man's wife couldn't be justified, even if they were both right and he would never return. So he stood at a distance and said nothing. Missy looked lost in her own home.

"It makes no sense," she went on. "We were both so excited to move here and make a new beginning. He never once questioned our choice. And now we're here, so why should he leave? Do you suppose he changed his mind for some reason and has gone back to our old neighborhood?"

"I don't know," Elisha replied, not very helpfully. It was, after all, not all that important why Compeyson had decided to leave. It was an immanent question, and therefore the answer, while it might seem dreadfully significant to Missy, wasn't really what this moment was all about. Compeyson's reason for leaving would not be the Author's reason for eliminating him, and the Author's reason mattered more. Still, in order to determine what that reason might be, Elisha needed to play this scene out to the end. "It could be, but why wouldn't he tell you? He must know that's the first place you'll look for him. If he's running away, that would not be a good place to hide, and if he's not, why wouldn't he tell you?"

"Exactly," Missy agreed. "It doesn't make any sense!" Elisha suspected it wasn't the last time she'd draw that conclusion this morning. But he had to agree with her. It made no sense to him, either. Previously, people had only dropped out of the story once their purpose had been accomplished. But what had Compeyson done that might be construed as fulfilling any sort of purpose? All he'd done since appearing in the story was drink coffee and eat cookies.

"Oh, I can't believe it!" Missy wailed. "What should I do?" She spun herself around, as though she had lost track of Elisha's whereabouts and didn't know which way to face while she turned to him in her desperation.

"What did the officer tell you?" Elisha asked, genuinely moved by Missy's tears and wishing he could help.

"Oh, he wasn't any help. He said that couples have spats all the time, and one of them leaves for a few hours or days to blow off steam, but that they nearly always return. So he said the police won't get involved until there's some clear indication of foul play.

"But we didn't have a spat. We both went to bed last night with a brand-new lease on life, feeling like the future was opening up before us and beckoning us to step into it. Sure, we're both a little befuddled about why it's happening, but Compeyson never expressed any regrets about the move or any anger at me for suggesting it. As far as I could tell, he was as happy here as I am. And then just like that, he vanishes entirely. I've never experienced anything like it. Have you, Elisha?"

He wasn't sure how to answer. Somehow, "Yes, last week one of my neighbors went up in smoke, and a customer of mine disappeared without a trace" seemed unlikely to comfort an abandoned wife and therefore better left unsaid. Instead he opted for a polite lie. "Well, you know, what the officer said makes a lot of sense, after all. Maybe something just set Compeyson off, and he needs time away to get his head on straight. After all, that story you two shared with me last night is a real humdinger." Elisha felt foolish using the word, but he was doing his best in a tough spot. "I bet you that he just needs time to himself to sort things out. I guess I wasn't very helpful last night, was I? He had serious questions, and I had no answers. He probably figured he needs to step away in order to think things through for himself." Elisha didn't believe it, but the least he could do for his distraught neighbor was to take the blame on himself. "Just wait, before long he'll come walking through your door and apologize for giving you such a fright."

Elisha knew he risked doing more harm than good in the long run by giving Missy false hope, but he'd make up for that the best he could later on. For now he could think of nothing better to say. The only possible alternative was the truth—that she and her husband were minor characters in someone else's story whose personal welfare took a back seat to the Author's true purpose—whatever that was. But it simply wouldn't do to reveal such a thing under these circumstances. She wouldn't believe it, for one thing, and even if by some unimaginable chance she did, then what? Elisha himself lacked answers to the questions that would inevitably follow. So where could such a conversation possibly lead? Nowhere good.

"What can I do, Missy? I'm worried for you. You shouldn't be left alone in your current state of mind. Would you like to come over to my place and visit for a while? That way you wouldn't have to spend the day in an empty house. Or if you'd prefer, I'd be willing to sit with you for a bit right here."

"Oh, Elisha!" Missy responded through grateful tears. "That's so thoughtful of you. I mean, we're practically strangers. I don't want to burden you with my own problems. That just wouldn't be neighborly," she said, trying to be light-hearted, but failing rather pathetically. "But I can't stand the thought of being alone. I mean, I suppose I'll have to learn to deal with it eventually, and that I'll have plenty of time to get good at it, but not just now. Not today, I mean. I just couldn't. So yes. Thank you, yes." Elisha didn't know whether she had just accepted his invitation to go home with him, or had invited him to stay with her. Feeling awkward, he waited for a clue what to do next. After a moment, she rose and declared, "I'll get my coat. I've had enough of boxes and unfinished rooms. It will be nice to spend the morning in a fully furnished, finished home."

Elisha sincerely hoped it would seem finished to her, even if it often felt otherwise to him. He couldn't help feeling terrible about what she must be going through, even if at some level it had been inevitable and necessary. He helped her put on her coat, took her tenderly by the arm, and led her toward the door. She leaned her head against his shoulder and followed submissively.

But before they reached the door, it swung open. Missy let out an involuntary cry of utter delight. Elisha cried out as well, but his cry was one of frightful astonishment bordering on shock—the sort of cry one makes upon seeing a ghost. In the open doorway stood Compeyson.

Missy and Elisha could tell that he'd been wearing a smile on his face, but it quickly vanished at the sight of his wife about to head out of the house in the arms of her new neighbor. "Where in the world are you two going?" he blurted out, his voice somewhere between an accusing growl and a sarcastic jest.

Elisha wilted, but Missy sprang at her husband, wrapped her arms around his neck, and burst into tears once more. He glanced over her shoulder toward Elisha with the annoyed look one wears when he's the only one in the room who doesn't get an inside joke. Elisha shrugged. "It's sure good to see you, Compeyson," he claimed, not at all sure whether it was in fact a good thing or a bad one.

"Will one of you please tell me what's going on?" Compeyson demanded.

"Oh, Compeyson," Missy sobbed. Or maybe she was laughing now. Elisha couldn't tell. "I thought you were gone."

"I was," her husband assured her.

"I know! But I mean, I thought you had left me. For good, that is. I woke up and you were nowhere to be found and I... well, I just jumped to conclusions, I guess. I've been a real mess. Elisha has been such a good neighbor. He was just offering me some friendship. All unnecessarily, I see now. Oh, honey, you don't know how happy I am to have you back home!" And with that Missy's sobs became uncontrollable, and she could say nothing more.

"For heaven's sake!" Compeyson swore. "Are you two out of your minds? I just headed out early this morning to check out Elisha's tip about that bank on Route 3. And it's a good thing I did, too. It turns out they need a new corporate loan officer, and I walked in at just the perfect moment. They gave me an interview and hired me on the spot. I start next Monday. I had intended to give you a well-deserved handshake, Elisha, but that was before I found you holding my wife by the hand." His tone and his expression had both softened, and Elisha could see that he was toying with him now that the misunderstanding had been explained. Elisha knew he must be turning red. He felt humiliated and for multiple reasons.

"I'm sorry," Compeyson apologized, now openly chuckling. "I can see I had both of you genuinely worried. I'm sorry I gave you a scare, but really! It never occurred to me for a second that anyone could imagine I'd walk out on my bride. And most certainly not now, when everything is beginning to fall into place and we're making a brand-new start."

Elisha estimated that his continued presence was neither needed nor especially desired, so he gave Compeyson a sheepish goodbye wave, wordlessly stepped around the embracing couple, and exited through the still-open door. He cursed his stupidity as he wandered back home. It was bad enough that he had been dead wrong about Compeyson; worse yet, the mistake left him without the slightest idea what to do next. Was this a rerun or wasn't it? Even if he could be sure of the answer, what course of action did it imply? He was tired of thinking about it and felt simply miserable.

Back in his kitchen, the dirty dishes in the sink seemed to be laughing at him, and he couldn't help thinking he deserved their mockery. They represented his life in microcosm: a job never finished, never even started for that matter. He could simply wash them and be done with it, of course, but that was hardly the real issue. The genuine dilemma was whether his story would go ever on or ever come to a resolution. He felt as he imagined Schrödinger's blasted cat must feel, neither dead nor alive, or maybe both, waiting for someone, anyone, to come and take a look at him so he'd know whether to go on breathing or start to rot. At this point, he'd accept either fate. But this endless not knowing where he was going or what he was supposed to do seemed destined to drive him mad. Doing the dishes couldn't help that. But it wouldn't hurt either, he supposed. He'd not succeeded in unraveling the mystery of his new neighbors or discovering his purpose, but he couldn't give up. He had to do something, and if he couldn't do something decisive or momentous, well then, he could at least do his dishes. And with that, he turned on the hot water tap and began filling the sink.

CHAPTER EIGHTEEN

Person of Interest

*One night the Lord spoke to Paul in a vision: "Do
not be afraid; keep on speaking, do not be silent. For
I am with you, and no one is going to attack and
harm you, because I have many people in this city."*
—*Acts 18:9–10*

Elisha had no sooner dried the last of his freshly cleaned glasses and returned it to its cupboard when he heard a loud knock at the door. Not bothering to remove his damp apron, he hurried to answer it, daring to imagine that he would open the door to find Mrs. Chancellor waiting on the other side. If Compeyson could return unexpectedly from oblivion, then perhaps his former neighbor would as well.

Elisha inhaled deeply and swung open the door. He didn't recognize the person facing him, but he knew instantly who he was and why he had come calling. The grave and serious man wore a tidy blue uniform with a silver badge on the breast. He also wore a belt around his waist fully equipped a holster and a pair of handcuffs. Elisha had no doubt that this man was quite capable of pinning him to the ground and securing his hands behind his back before he even realized what was happening or dared to protest. "Good morning, Officer," he said. "What can I do for you?"

"Are you the owner—Mr. Elisha Bookbinder?"

"That's right," Elisha felt compelled to acknowledge, because inconvenient as the fact seemed at the present moment, that's exactly who he was. "What can I do for you?" he repeated.

"May I come inside?"

Elisha concluded that the officer would share information according to his own agenda, but apparently not in response to unsolicited questions. He wondered what would happen if he denied the request, which was the answer he desperately wanted to give, but decided it would do no good. Rather, he guessed it was exactly what the officer hoped he would do, if only so that he could produce a warrant and triumphantly disregard Elisha's wishes.

"Please do," Elisha answered as cheerfully as he could. The policeman stepped through the door and Elisha closed it behind him. As the officer passed, Elisha took careful note of the badge in order to ascertain his identity: Patrolman 41707. "Have a seat," Elisha offered, motioning toward the sofa.

"No, thank you, sir. I'm here to ask a few questions, if you don't mind." Elisha didn't really expect that it made the least bit of difference whether he minded or not but, again, he didn't test his assumption by objecting.

"Is this about my next-door neighbor?" He asked.

"Yes, sir. His disappearance."

"But he didn't disappear," Elisha objected. "Not really, anyway. He just stepped out for a couple of hours to go job hunting, and he didn't tell his wife. She jumped to conclusions when she woke up and couldn't find him. Well, we both did, I guess. But he returned just about an hour ago. It was all just a misunderstanding. No harm done."

"Is that so?"

"It is. I just returned from there. I'd gone over to console the wife when I saw the police car in the driveway. I assume that was you?" Patrolman 41707 offered no clarification. Clearly, he intended to do all the questioning and get all the answers; not the other way around. Elisha continued. "By the time I headed out, Compeyson was in his wife's arms, and she was crying for joy."

"Then you have no explanation for why they are both missing?"

"Missing? That can't be," Elisha objected. "Like I said, I left them safe and sound barely an hour ago."

"Not so," challenged the officer. "I was just there myself. No one answered the doorbell, and I knocked my knuckles raw. There's no one there."

Elisha wasn't impressed. "That may be, but I'm sure they just headed out to a late breakfast after all the commotion they had this morning. Or maybe to the mall to buy some curtains or such. They're just moving in, you know. They're from out of state."

"Yes, I know that, sir." It seemed to Elisha that the interview wasn't getting very far and was pointless to begin with, but the officer nevertheless scribbled in his notepad each time Elisha spoke, as if his words might prove to be the vital clue needed to solve some great mystery.

"Oh," Elisha replied. "Well, anyway, there must be two dozen likely explanations for why they were unable to answer the door. Surely there's no reason to suspect anything nefarious."

The officer gave no indication that he cared to hear Elisha's theories. "Is it true," he asked in a monotone voice, "that just last week, you told a first responder that you were responsible for the death of one Mrs. Chancellor, who then resided at the very same address as your missing neighbors?"

Elisha felt a chill. There apparently was more to this interrogation than he'd expected. He sensed great danger, and the need to answer this and future questions much more cautiously than he had so far. "Am I being accused of something?" he demanded. "Should I get a lawyer?"

"No, sir, that won't be necessary. Not at this time at least. I'm just here to gather some facts. There have been some odd goings-on of late, and you're what we call a person of interest. If you are innocent, you have nothing to worry about."

Elisha felt not the least bit reassured. "Innocent of what, exactly? I already told you that my neighbors are both safe and sound, or at least they were when I last left them. And yes, I did suggest to Graham Ripper—he's the EMT—that I may have contributed to Mrs. Chancellor's demise, but I was quite frantic when I said it and not thinking all that clearly. Ripper himself told me that no one was to blame. Those were his exact words. He even suggested that I seek counseling. And I did. That's how crazy he thought my claim was. And I no longer feel guilty about causing her death. She died of spontaneous combustion. That was the official conclusion. So why am I suddenly a suspect?"

"You aren't," Patrolman 41707 repeated unconvincingly. "I'm just asking a few routine questions. Tell me though, do you have any knowledge of a gentleman by the name of Drew Unwin?"

Elisha said nothing. His mind raced. He imagined two dozen likely outcomes of this interrogation, and he didn't like a single one of them.

"Do you, sir?" the policeman repeated.

"What makes you ask that?" Elisha croaked. He couldn't fathom how they'd made the connection. He'd only met the man the one time and talked to him once on the phone.

"Do you, sir?"

"Well, yes, sort of. I mean, we weren't friends or even casual associates. He was a customer of mine last week. But I haven't seen him since." Elisha thought that last bit might help distance himself from Unwin and allow him to convincingly answer "I don't know" to any subsequent requests for information.

"Neither has anyone else, it turns out," replied Officer 41707 in a grave voice. Elisha's heart sank. "But neighbors reported seeing someone fitting your description poking around his house." Elisha's heart sank even lower, but it wasn't a question, so he didn't feel obligated to say anything more.

"What was the nature of your relationship?"

"Like I said, he was a customer," Elisha offered. "I own a bookshop. He called me last week offering to sell me a vintage copy of the works of Shakespeare. But we never closed the deal. That's all."

"This edition of Shakespeare, Mr. Bookbinder—might it have been an 1880 leather-bound copy published by Ginn & Company?"

"Exactly, but—"

The officer interrupted Elisha before he could finish. "We found it in his living room, covered with two sets of fingerprints. One set belongs to Mr. Unwin. Would you like to tell us who the other set belongs to?"

Elisha swallowed hard. "Those would be mine, I imagine. Unwin handed me the book when he visited my shop, and I handled it quite thoroughly. I mean, I was considering a purchase and so naturally I had to examine it."

"Naturally," the officer said, again writing furiously in his notepad. "But it does place your fingerprints in the home of a missing person, doesn't it? Were you there, Mr. Bookbinder?"

Elisha once again considered the advisability of engaging a lawyer, but he didn't want to seem combative or uncooperative. As frightening as the interview had become, he knew he remained perfectly innocent of any wrongdoing—other than trespassing, perhaps—and reasoned that truth remained the wisest strategy. For now, anyway. "Yes, I was. Briefly. I visited him to finish our business with the book. But Unwin was already gone when I arrived."

"Then why didn't you report his disappearance?"

"It never seemed necessary," Elisha said. "His front door was standing open, so I assumed he'd gone for a walk, that's all." Truth was useful, he reasoned, but like many things in life, it's possible to overdo it. "I had no compelling reason to think the police needed to get involved. People are still allowed to go for a walk, aren't they?" It was a foolish thing to say, Elisha knew, but his annoyance with the investigation was beginning to outpace his fear.

"Is that *Storm on the Sea of Galilee?*" Patrolman 41707 asked, jutting a thumb in the direction of the fireplace.

"It's a reproduction," Elisha insisted.

"Uh-huh." The officer scribbled on for a few more minutes in silence, then observed, "Trouble does seem to follow you around, doesn't it, Mr. Bookbinder? Do you have anything to add?"

Elisha felt a glimmer of hope. The questions seemed to be nearly at an end, and this last one was the easiest of them all: "No, that's everything."

"So you have nothing to say about the man who was impaled by a telephone pole practically on your doorstep last week? The one who seems to have had no prior history before turning up dead just after leaving your house?" Elisha dropped his head into his hands and noticed it had begun to ache. "Why don't you start at the beginning, Mr. Bookbinder, and tell me everything." Elisha imagined a touch of gloating in his voice, as if he'd successfully sprung a cleverly laid trap—or was it more than just his imagination? "I'm sure it will be a most interesting story," the man in blue said, "and I'm anxious to hear it. Or would you prefer that I took you down to the station and have you tell it to me there?"

In the several seconds of silence that ensued, Elisha almost thought he heard a distant voice—Christopher's—saying: "You have not been given the ability to convince people of the truth, I'm afraid. But you will have to tell them nevertheless."

And so it was. He had no choice. None. He'd been backed into a corner, and the only way out was straight ahead. This was the time for his great revelation. He would utterly fail, of course, to persuade this officer of what was real and who Christopher was. No matter. That wasn't his purpose. Or so he'd been assured. This was just another step on the long journey toward that purpose. But exactly what it might be remained out of sight beyond a far horizon.

"Well, all right then," he told the officer. "But it's quite a long story. I really do think you ought to sit down."

CHAPTER NINETEEN

Overexposed

This is the verdict: Light has come into the world, but men
loved darkness instead of light because their deeds were
evil. Everyone who does evil hates the light, and will not
come into the light for fear that his deeds will be exposed.
—John 3:19–20

E lisha had to smile despite his narrow escape. Knowing before-
hand that nothing he said could possibly convince Patrolman
41707 of the incredible truth had the happy effect of reliev-
ing Elisha of the burden of responsibility he might otherwise have
felt, and whatever his true purpose might be, knowing that convert-
ing his interrogator to his own point of view did not enter into it
allowed him to embrace the sheer absurdity of this encounter, and
relish it. If Patrolman 41707 had at the outset felt triumphant over
trapping Elisha into confessing the extent of his involvement in
the strange occurrences surrounding the cases of Mrs. Chancellor,
Unwin, Christopher, and Compeyson, then Elisha enjoyed the
last laugh all that much more. He shared everything, in the most
exquisite detail, noting with great pleasure that partway through his
intricate account, the officer stopped asking probing questions, and
ceased taking notes. Indeed, he seemed most impatient for Elisha to

162

get to the end of his outlandish story so he could leave. But Elisha simply wouldn't end. He enjoyed his little game too much for that. He could tell that the man in blue sitting across from him (he had indeed helped himself to a seat about the time Elisha got to the part about Schrödinger's cat) thought him partly insane, but not criminally so, which was the perfect outcome in Elisha's judgment. Having achieved it, he could now playfully pay the officer back for his earlier sarcastic insistence that Elisha "tell him everything."

The sun had dipped below the western horizon before Elisha ran out of things to say and reluctantly announced to his exasperated guest that "that just about covers everything." But just to rub it in he added, "Any more questions?"

"No, that should do it," his stunned guest assured him. "My shift will be over before long. I need to get back to the station and file my report."

"By the way, sir," Elisha added with grave seriousness, "would you by any chance know the name of Pavlov's dog?"

"W-w-who? What?" Patrolman 41707 stammered. "Ah, no. No I don't. Good evening Mr. Bookbinder. I'll be in touch." But Elisha was dead certain he wouldn't. The officer turned, and he hurried out the door without remembering to thank Elisha for the many leads he had provided. He climbed briskly into his patrol car, backed quickly out of the driveway, and very nearly collided with Compeyson and Missy, who were just returning from the mall with some new draperies. Elisha managed to close the door again before laughing out loud. All in all, it had been a fine day, and more fun that he'd had in a good, long time. He'd never before been a terror to anyone, and he found his new power perversely intoxicating. He hadn't anticipated this side of things.

He had imagined that his discovery, not to mention the equally unforeseen encounter with the Author himself, might leave his acquaintances incredulous, but simple disbelief couldn't adequately explain either Huxley's response to Elisha's account, nor the patrol-man's. He'd seen something more powerful than mere skepticism in their eyes—something closer to despair or even fright. Not the sort of fear one experiences when faced with physical dangers, but more like a dread of the unknown and unknowable. Both Huxley and Patrolman 41707 had reacted as if their very manhood had been drained away, and a childish dread of liver and sauerkraut, a dish they had never tried, had overwhelmed them.

Elisha found it puzzling and simply couldn't empathize. For all the angst his discovery had unleashed within his soul—the doubts, the myriad questions, the palpable sense of an unseen presence, the self-conscious desire to know the truth coupled with an equal but opposite wish to remain blissfully ignorant—he had never once felt in his soul that thing he had so clearly seen in Huxley's eyes, and now in those of the patrolman. He hadn't felt pure, unbridled revul-sion. He'd swung back and forth between belief and disbelief, and had even questioned the Author's motives but never had the possi-bility of his presence struck Elisha as intrinsically repellent. And so it quite simply astonished him that others might react so. A new truth dawned in Elisha's mind—the presence of the Author was not so much unbelievable to some, as simply unwelcome.

He wondered whether it amounted to a good or a bad thing, this intense aversion some people seemingly had for their Creator. Certainly, it could be used to his advantage; he'd just demonstrated that by using it to send an unwanted visitor on his way as if the hounds of hell were nipping at his heals and his eternal soul depended upon making a hasty, undignified escape. But though he'd enjoyed a laugh at the poor patrolman's expense, Elisha knew in his heart that it had been an unworthy and selfish game on his part. Christopher him-self, he felt certain, would not have laughed along with him, despite having a playful side of his own. More likely, Christopher would have reminded him that everyone has a purpose, Elisha mused. The officer had merely been pursuing his. And in the meantime, Elisha's own purpose remained unaccomplished. The story that seemed so near an end kept going on, and might continue to do so endlessly if Elisha couldn't wrap things up. But what remained to be done? He wished Christopher would place the necessary details into his head, the way he placed orange juice in his refrigerator. But some things, apparently, Elisha had to figure out himself. Why? He couldn't guess. And guessing, he instinctively knew, wasn't the right approach. He needed to be sure.

So he took a more analytical approach and began making a mental list. Everyone had a purpose, Christopher had assured him. Everyone. But that purpose, Elisha noted, too often became apparent only after it had been accomplished and that person had dropped out of the story. Unwin had been the first to accomplish his purpose, although his departure from the story remained unnoticed for a short while. Then Mrs. Chancellor had fulfilled her destiny and dropped out. Her departure had been impossible to overlook. Christopher, uniquely, had predicted his own departure, but then he too walked off the stage just like all the rest. Were there any others? Though it remained to be seen, Elisha felt confident that Patrolman 41707 would not return.

Folks just don't seem to hang around very long in this story, Elisha thought. *Except me. I just keep on going and going, never drawing any nearer to my ultimate destination.*

But no, that wasn't quite right, he realized. He wasn't the only one. There were others whose part hadn't yet ended. There was Compeyson and Missy, of course, whose late arrival and uncertain role had him befuddled. And then there was Huxley. He had another appointment with Huxley in just two days. What would come of it? Earlier in the week, Elisha had assumed the story would end before the appointment rolled around, but so far, that hadn't happened, and now the end didn't seem nearly so imminent. So Huxley, it appeared, hadn't fulfilled his purpose either.

Then there was Graham Ripper. Elisha couldn't decide what to make of him. Graham seemed to turn up only when needed to help escort fallen heroes off the stage. So as long as characters continued to work toward unfinished goals, he was liable to be needed again. Elisha expected he'd turn up from time to time. But as his purpose appeared to be merely garbage disposal, Elisha left him out of his reckoning as a key to resolving his story's plot.

Whom did that leave? In his head, Elisha relived the events that had transpired since Unwin stepped into his bookshop. He wasn't sure that's the exact point at which his story began, but prior to that he'd not met or interacted with anyone of particular note for quite a long time—since before his strange "unfinished" sensations had begun. Rather arbitrarily, he decided that he needn't think back any farther than that. That left only the folks he'd encountered at the Christmas Eve church service, and the young philosophy student who had been delighted to find a copy of *Being and Nothingness* earlier in the week. Elisha mentally struck her off his list as well, reasoning that there were many, many ways to drop out of a story, and while the young woman had neither been incinerated, vanished mysteriously, or been impaled, finding *Nothingness* amounted to pretty much the same thing, at least in a poetic sense. In addition, he still believed that events in recent days were somehow a rerun of things he had experienced the previous week. If that was so, then the student's visit to the bookshop represented a rerun of Unwin's similar visit. And that had been the last time Elisha ever saw Unwin. Of course, he'd been embarrassingly off-base when he'd employed similar logic to deduce Compeyson's disappearance, so it wouldn't pay to rely too heavily on such reasoning, but on the whole, it seemed most likely that he'd seen the last of the young student as well.

Elisha began to feel as though he was gaining a handle on things. At the very least, a plan of action began to take shape in his mind. Of all the characters who'd played a role in his unfinished story, only his new neighbors, Huxley, and Pastor Preston Johns seemed likely to have any unfinished business with him. He'd meet again with each of them, in turn, in the hope of giving each the opportunity to fulfill their purposes. Perhaps by doing so, not only would they tie up their loose ends, but more importantly, Elisha's own purpose would become clearer.

He'd see Huxley first. He'd already made an appointment, so that seemed like the best place to begin. And he already had a good idea how that interview would go; it was the most predictable of the three necessary conversations. It wouldn't be all that much different from the interview he'd just had with Patrolman 41707, except that Huxley, he felt sure, would protest more vehemently during the conversation, raising objections to oppose Elisha's bold declarations. And along the way, he'd say something that had been left unsaid during Elisha's first session with him, or in some other way achieve his purpose. Or at least that was Elisha's hope and expectation.

After that he'd make an appointment with Preston Johns. Elisha had far less of an idea how that talk might go. Presumably, the pastor would be more open to the idea of a Creative Presence behind the world than the clinical psychologist, but he might balk at the idea that such a force was not God but only a second-rate writer. Things could get sticky when Elisha shared that part of his revelation, but maybe he could talk his way around it.

Finally, he'd have to arrange for another visit with Compeyson and Missy. Maybe he'd invite them over to his place this time. Repaying them for their hospitality would make a good excuse for another get-together. But he'd save that interview for last. He'd already been wracking his brain for two days trying to figure out their role. He needed a break before delving back into that aspect of his story once again.

For the first time in longer than he could remember, Elisha had a long-term plan of action. Rather than reacting to events, now at last he'd be dictating them. He felt good about himself again. His story was back in his own hands. Well, in part, at least. He would no longer wait and see. Now, if not exactly a creator, he could at least lay claim to being something of a subcreator. It was a fresh start.

CHAPTER TWENTY

Alternative Facts

*"Do not give dogs what is sacred; do not throw your
pearls to pigs. If you do, they may trample them under
their feet, and then turn and tear you to pieces."*
—*Matthew 7:6*

A week had passed since Huxley had reminded his patient that
they had another session "same time next week" as Elisha
had run from the psychologist's office. At the time, Elisha
had intended to break the appointment, but one week later, he found
himself anxious to bring the therapist up to date and hear his reac-
tions. He imagined it ought to be instructive, if not entirely decisive.

The receptionist ushered Elisha into Huxley's office, invited
him to make himself comfortable, and left him to wait for the doctor
to arrive. Huxley seemed in no great hurry, and Elisha passed the
time perusing the several impressive diplomas, certificates of membership to prestigious societies, and awards that decorated the walls.
It struck Elisha that the therapist had much more at stake when it
came to evaluating this case than Elisha had appreciated the first
time the two had met. Then, he had chided Huxley for clearly dis-
liking Elisha's worldview and desperately wanting to refute it. Now
he began to understand why that should be. It would be wrong to

attribute it to mere intellectual stubbornness. The consequences of being proven wrong would turn Huxley's world upside down no less than the consequences of being proven right had overturned Elisha's own. He had come to this session relishing the thought of putting the doctor in his place, but as he stood before these many testaments to a life devoted to the pursuit of honors Elisha's revelations would render irrelevant, Elisha pitied Huxley and empathized. They will not accept it, Christopher had assured him, and suddenly Elisha saw why it would always be so. Would he have been any different had his circumstances and Huxley's been reversed?—if he were the highly successful professional with so much to lose and Huxley merely an old-fashioned shopkeeper for whom escaping into imaginary worlds constituted a pleasant means of savoring adventures he could experience in no other way?

Huxley had been right after all—in one respect anyway. And so had Elisha. Wish fulfillment played a big part in forming the beliefs of both. That's why the very same evidence could point one of them in this direction and the other in that, and why no amount of evidence would ever make them see things the same way. But even so, neither wishing for something nor desperately wanting it to be false could ever change what was real. In the end, while both might want to be proven correct, only one of them was. And for the other, what? A life spent in pursuit of a mirage. The stakes couldn't be higher, Elisha solemnly concluded, regardless of which way one's wishes pointed. He regretted toying with Officer 41707's emotions. Whatever his ultimate purpose might be, he doubted that it involved pleasing himself at the expense of others. And yet, that would inevitably be the result of every effort to put forth the truth with any conviction. And that was precisely what Elisha was here for.

Huxley finally entered, breaking Elisha's ruminations. "Elisha, I'm pleased to see you. And a little surprised. The way in which you left our session last week had me thinking I wouldn't see you again."

Elisha smiled apologetically. "I had some questions that needed answering, and answers I needed to question. But this wasn't the place to ask them, and you weren't the one I needed to talk to."

"Who was?"

"I was."

"So you've been talking to yourself this past week?"

"Among others. But yes, I have."

"And what have you learned?" Huxley prompted.

Elisha took that as an indication that the session had officially begun. He sat facing Huxley, placed his elbows on the arms of the Burgundy-colored leather chair facing Huxley's desk, and touched the tips of his fingers together before him. He well understood that Huxley's job would be to get him to open up so as to reveal his inner demons. Elisha hosted none at the moment, but fully intended to open up regardless. He was paying good money for this session and didn't want to squander the opportunity.

"Dr. Huxley, the last time we spoke you assured me that there are ideas that don't require formal proofs because practical experience has shown them to be reliable. I think perhaps I was too quick to dismiss that argument." Elisha paused, curious to hear how Huxley reacted to the admission.

"Go on," the therapist replied. So he was going to be allowed to tell his story his own way, Elisha concluded. Perhaps Huxley too had done some soul searching following their previous contentious encounter.

"You also very astutely inquired as to whether I'd been hearing voices," Elisha noted.

"And I was encouraged to hear that you hadn't." Huxley was taking notes now, just as Patrolman 41707 had done during his interview. Elisha noted with some amusement that for someone that nobody believed, folks sure did take an interest in what he had to say. Elisha wondered at what point Huxley might give up, as his predecessor had done. "Yes, I could see that at the time," Elisha responded. "But your question got me thinking. If my theory was true, why shouldn't I hear from the Author? And yet I hadn't. Until you mentioned it, the idea hadn't even occurred to me. It was an inconsistency in my own story that demanded an explanation, although it admittedly took me quite some time to realize it."

"But now you have."

"Yes, the Author's silence could mean only one thing, namely, that I was wrong."

"You see that now?" Huxley confirmed.

"Very clearly. Which is why I'm so very pleased that he did."

"Did what?"

"Spoke to me. Well, dropped by for breakfast, to be more accurate. He is a man, by the way. The last time we talked I had not yet determined that, as I recall." Huxley continued writing with only a barely perceptible flinch, Elisha saw. He was impressed. "And so you see," he concluded, "the Author's existence is now a matter of practical experience and must be accepted as proven, for all intents and purposes. He has helped me to overcome doubt and reach sound 'conclusions,' as you yourself said so well. And after all, a mirage doesn't leave behind a sink full of dirty dishes."

Elisha paused to allow Huxley time to say, "Do continue," or "You don't say," or some other equally non-committal encouragement to keep talking, but the therapist said nothing. "I just thought you ought to know," Elisha concluded.

Huxley looked as if he had something he very much needed to say and which he wanted at all costs to avoid saying. Elisha waited patiently while two impulses—one clinical, the other personal—vied for supremacy inside Huxley's head. Several long moments passed before Huxley asked haltingly, "What did he say?"

"That it would be futile to try to convince you, but that I should tell my story nonetheless. It seemed pointless to me at the time, but I think maybe I'm beginning to understand. You see, it's not really about you in the end. It's about me. Telling you about the Author won't change your outlook. Your outlook is fixed, and even if he were to appear to you as he did to me, you wouldn't accept it. You can't. I quite understand that now. But I suppose talking about it has something to do with my own purpose, which I'm still trying to figure out. That's why I came back for this session. To talk, and then see where it leads."

"You say you've found evidence that proves your theory, but that it's unconvincing to anyone but you. Doesn't that strike you as suspicious? Why shouldn't others be persuaded, if your evidence is really so convincing?"

"Because you have it all backwards," Elisha replied. "You make the assumption, as most people do, that they are motivated by pure, unbiased reason. They sincerely believe, as you do, that their beliefs are the result of factual analysis."

"But you disagree?"

"Your words and actions fail to support that interpretation," Elisha explained. "Your thinking really works in quite the opposite direction. You haven't arrived at a conclusion based on evidence. You have no desire to. Instead, you've selected a conclusion that satisfies you on an emotional level, and you defend it against all evidence to the contrary. If the facts don't support your desired outcome, you simply exchange them for alternate facts more to your liking. The more evidence I bring against your worldview, the less likely you are to accept it, because it threatens the security you find in a belief system that provides you with a greater sense of autonomy. I can sympathize with that. There must be all sorts of emotional reasons for refusing to consider the Author's reality. Freedom from any rules he might impose, for example. Another reason could be a desire to be your own boss, and a corresponding distaste for the whole notion that there is something farther back and higher up that has a claim on you. Or maybe it's simpler than all that. It could just be the natural human tendency to despise anyone more talented, more creative, and more wise than we are. People like that make us feel comparatively unimportant. Who needs that? In contrast to any of these exceptional reasons for banishing the Author from our thinking, all I have to offer is cold evidence. And yes, it works the other way around too. I am no less governed by emotion. But in my worldview emotions are a valid source of input. In your worldview they are not; rather, they are dismissed as mere distractions. So while my reason is informed by my emotions, you can only suppress them and deny their existence. But you can't destroy them. They lurk just beyond conscious thought, influencing your every argument just like the Author whose existence terrifies you."

Huxley had risen from his chair as Elisha spoke and begun pacing rapidly. Now he took a seat next to his patient, but Elisha himself rose and without further comment, took a seat behind Huxley's desk.

"Nonsense. Sheer and utter nonsense," Huxley muttered.

"Tell me why you feel it to be nonsense," Elisha asked quite professionally.

"There is no evidence. Not a shred."

"I shared breakfast with the man."

"Why should I believe such drivel?"

"Tell me more about these doubts of yours. And your fears."

Huxley looked as though he might wretch. "I'm not afraid!"

"Is that true?" Elisha asked kindly.

"Yes! Yes! It's true!" Huxley shouted.

"Good. I can see that you are finally getting in touch with your emotions. I think we've made some good progress today."

Huxley began sobbing uncontrollably as the receptionist, alarmed by his cries, burst through the door. "What's happening in here? Are you all right, sir?" she asked with some alarm, even before catching the sight of Huxley curled up in a chair, hands over his ears and eyes screwed shut, crying. "Oh, my heavens!" she exclaimed. "What can I do for you, sir?"

"You probably ought to call Graham Ripper," Elisha suggested. "He knows people who can help in situations such as this. I believe you'll find his number in in your Rolodex." He rose from Huxley's chair. "I don't think we'll need to schedule any further follow-ups. Wouldn't you say so, Huxley?" The therapist nodded vigorously. Elisha thanked the startled receptionist and excused himself. "No charge," he assured Huxley as he took his leave.

Once outside the office, Elisha's mood grew more serious. He'd successfully refuted Huxley, but he'd gotten no closer to understanding his purpose. Ultimately, this had been a dead end. But other options remained, places where he might possibly find his answer, and people who might provide them. One down, two to go. Next, he'd visit someone for whom an unseen Author ought not to seem emotionally unacceptable.

CHAPTER TWENTY ONE

The Realm of Preston Johns

"Who is this that darkens my counsel
with words without knowledge?"
—Job 38:2

E lisha rapped lightly at Reverend Preston Johns' office door, not at all sure what to expect from his visit. He told himself not to get his hopes up, but that quite naturally proved difficult.

"Enter," called a voice from the other side. Elisha obeyed. "Shoes," the same voice intoned.

"I beg your pardon," Elisha said. "What shoes?"

"Your shoes," the pastor clarified. "Take them off please and leave them by the door. Right there next to mine."

Sure enough, just inside the door sat a pair of brown leather wing tips, side by side with their laces tucked inside. Elisha said nothing, but sat on the sofa facing the pastor's desk and undid his own laces.

"New carpet," the pastor explained. "We're trying to avoid unnecessary wear. I guess you didn't see the sign outside the door."

"No, I didn't. My mistake," Elisha apologized politely, without really feeling guilty of anything requiring repentance.

With an air of overstated dignity, Johns dismissed the oversight with a wave of his hand, as if he were granting a stay of execution. "Don't feel bad. Everybody misses it. I'll have to propose to the Board that we make a bigger sign. In the meantime, I don't object to reminding folks."

"Thank you," Elisha offered.

"Don't mention it." If Elisha wasn't mistaken, he saw the pastor place a small check mark next to the first item on a handwritten list laying before him. The writing was upside down from Elisha's perspective and too small for him to easily read, but the word on the first line was of just the right length to be "shoes."

"Well, anyway, please do sit down. It's Elisha, isn't it? I don't believe we've ever had the chance to talk personally, but I recognize the name from your offering envelope. Tell me, how did you like the Christmas Eve message?"

"It got me thinking," Elisha answered without embellishment.

"Oh? Well, that's good. What about, exactly?"

"Mostly about Herod. I wondered how I might have fared if I were in his shoes, not knowing what the future held or whether the Wise Men were of God, or agents intent on stirring up an insurrection, or maybe even the vanguard of a foreign invasion." Elisha didn't bother to say that at the present moment, he wondered how it would feel to be in *anybody's* shoes.

Pastor Johns whistled. "My word, you *are* a deep thinker aren't you? That never occurred to me, I assure you. All I meant to do was recite the Christmas story. There was no deeper meaning behind it."

"Behind the Christmas story?" It struck Elisha as an odd thing for his pastor to say.

"Yes. Still, that's part of the Bible's charm, isn't it? We all take something different away from it. It speaks to us in a variety of ways and each of us hears a unique personal message in its words."

"I suppose. Although right now, I'm less interested in what I might hear than in what the Author intended to convey."

"Who's to say?" Johns asked. "Well, anyway, I'm glad we have this opportunity to get better acquainted. What is it that you wanted to talk about? My secretary tells me you made this appointment to ask my advice about some personal decisions facing you, but she says you declined to go into any details over the phone."

"I didn't mean to be mysterious," Elisha assured his pastor, not entirely honestly. "It's just that it's hard to put my thoughts into words, and I thought I'd avoid the bother of having to explain myself twice."

"Well, it's just the two of us now, Elisha, so why don't you tell me how I can help you?"

"I appreciate that, Pastor." Elisha gathered himself for what he hoped would be a pivotal revelation. "It's all about finding my purpose. I have this sense that I'm being called to something…"

"Ah, and you're considering whether or not the ministry is a viable option?" Johns interjected.

"Oh no, it's nothing like that," Elisha chuckled. "I'm not contemplating ordination. But there are many roles we might play and I'm curious about how I might go about finding mine. It's like Shakespeare said, 'All the world's a stage, and all the men and women merely players.' Everyone has a part to play. Wouldn't you agree?"

"Ah, yes! So you want to know where you can plug in. That's quite commendable, and we encourage all our members to take an active part in one or more of our ministries. The first thing we'll have you do is take a gifts survey. Then after we've identified your talents, I can introduce you to some of our staff and they can explain our programs to you. Are you a musician, by any chance? Our keyboardist left us recently. He was quite popular and membership has been declining since he—"

"No, it's nothing like that," Elisha interrupted. "I'm thinking more about my role outside the church, in my everyday life."

"Even better!" Johns exulted. "We take pride in preaching social relevance. We understand that everyone has felt needs, and we're committed to equipping today's Christian to pursue his dreams and live life abundantly, whether they chose to pursue happiness through marriage or as a single, through social activism or political awareness. You've come to the right church if you're seeking a resource to serve your personal ambitions."

Elisha weighed the pastor's words. "No, that doesn't quite hit the nail on the head either. I'm thinking of something more, um, transcendent."

"I'm not sure I understand," the pastor confessed. "Helping people help themselves is the heartbeat of modern ministry. It's what today's generation craves. That and interactive community. So we scratch that itch for them. It's the foundation for all we do."

"Really?" asked Elisha, genuinely surprised.

"Of course. We live in a rapidly changing, exciting world, Elisha. But of course, that comes with its own challenges. We're entering a new age, a postmodern renaissance brimming with new freedoms, new opportunities, and new definitions of truth. Once everything shakes out, probably in a generation or two, we'll hardly recognize things. We're in a major paradigm shift. But for now, it's got people feeling disoriented. Everything's in flux, from who our enemies are to which toilet we can use. People are desperate for guidance and more and more, we're who they turn to. That gives us a great opportunity to be relevant once again. For a while there, during the post-war years, people had given up on the church. We've had to reinvent ourselves in order to give folks what today's generation really wants—self-confidence, self-determination, and self-satisfaction."

"And self-righteousness?" Elisha proposed with a hint of sarcasm. "Well, I wouldn't word it quite that way. Let's call it self-sufficiency. But yes, that's the essence of it. So you see, Elisha, these questions you've been asking about where life is taking you are perfectly normal. Everyone is asking them these days, but rest assured, we've got answers for you."

Elisha felt disoriented. The dialog had taken an entirely unanticipated direction. "Pastor," he started over. "I'm not looking to find myself. I don't need a purpose, I've already got one. I just need to understand what it is. I'm wondering why I'm here, what I was created for. Does the Bible tell us anything about our God-given purpose, either as a community or individually? I believe I was made for a specific reason and that so far, I've neglected it. It nags at me, and I need to know what's expected of me so I can submit myself to my Creator and please him by fulfilling his expectations for me. I know—or at least I assume—that the Bible doesn't address my own personal situation, but I thought there must be clues in there about what we were made for and how to please our Creator." That, Elisha hoped, explained the reason for his visit clearly enough to avoid further misunderstandings.

"The Bible?" Johns asked, not certain he was following Elisha's train of thought.

"Yes," Elisha affirmed. "I was led to believe some authoritative instruction might be found here."

"Oh, yes, well for sure," Johns allowed. "You must understand, though, that the Bible is an ancient document, and as such, it doesn't directly address the needs of our current generation."

"It does tell us about creation and our relationship to the Creator, though, doesn't it?"

"Certainly. But it's primarily inspirational. You can't take it literally. Its creation stories—there are two of them you know—are meant to inspire us to have trust in God's goodness and faith in the ultimate victory of good over evil, but you can't rely on them to dictate how we should live our lives. That's for each of us to work out for ourselves. 'Seek out your salvation with fear and trembling,' that's what the Bible says."

"That's all?" Elisha felt deflated.

"Pretty much. Along with the assurance that all who seek it will ultimately find true happiness."

"It seems like it takes an awful lot of verbiage to tell a very simple story if that's all there is to it," Elisha noted.

"I'll tell you what, Elisha. I can see you're still skeptical. Here, why don't you take this. We give it to all our Seekers. It'll point you in the right direction, you'll see." Johns handed Elisha a booklet titled *The Seven Habits of Completely Contented Christians.* He quickly scanned the contents. Page 1 bore the heading "Marking Your Territory" and was followed by a section titled "Inviting God to Join Your Team."

"I appreciate this," Elisha lied, "but I don't know. It doesn't really seem to be what I'm looking for."

"Well, give it a chance," Johns insisted. "Our new members swear by it. Most of them anyway," he clarified. "Every now and then we get a literalist who tells us all we need to pray more, or get right with God." He chuckled.

"Literalists?" Elisha asked with renewed interest. "Would it be possible to talk with any of them?"

"Well, no," Johns admitted, with slight embarrassment. "They tend to leave without notice and don't often stay in touch, so... well, no."

Then Johns' expression grew brighter and he sat up straighter, as if he'd received some divine inspiration. "Say! You're single, aren't you, Elisha? Of course you are! Why didn't I think of this until now? We have a singles support group. Why don't you come out for it? I'll bet that would go a long way towards satisfying your felt need. You could use some companionship I'll bet, and that group is a good place to find community. They meet once a week to share stories and do life together."

With a start, Elisha realized that he would never find answers in this seemingly most promising of places. The Author constituted just as great an inconvenience for Johns as he did for Huxley. Though each saw the world in very different ways, neither had room in their worldview for a Prime Mover whose purposes might overrule their own agenda. The very notion had brought Huxley to tears, and if he pressed the issue much further, Elisha might easily have the same unfortunate effect on this man of God who required visitors to check their soles at the door.

"Well," Elisha stalled, "I'll consider what your good book has to say—the pamphlet, I mean." He began to wish that his purpose was to lie in church, because he felt he was becoming rather good at it. "I appreciate your time and your advice, Pastor, but I don't want to keep you any longer. I expect that you must have big plans for tonight."

It was December 31.

"Yes, I do. Happily, most of my kids and their families live locally. We all get together each year for a dinner and some fireworks. You?"

"Not me. I prefer just to watch a little television before retiring early. It's just another evening as far as that goes."

"Well, to each his own. I do hope you find what you're looking for, Elisha, I really do. Please remember the singles group."

"I won't forget," Elisha assured him. But by the time his shoes were back on his feet, he had. Everyone had a purpose, Christopher had said.

Well, Elisha thought, *I suppose some people's role is to be utterly useless.*

He exited the church wondering what sort of unfortunate fireworks accident Graham Ripper might have to respond to before the evening was over.

CHAPTER TWENTY TWO

Across the Multiverse

*The time will come when men will not
put up with sound doctrine.
Instead, to suit their own desires, they
will gather around them
a great number of teachers to say what
their itching ears want to hear.
They will turn their ears away from the
truth and turn aside to myths.*
—2 Timothy 4:3–4

The last sun of the old year had already dipped below the western horizon by the time Elisha re-emerged from his talk with Pastor Johns. He tramped back home dejectedly, depressed by his unexpected failure to find meaningful answers in a church. There had been some friendly encouragement, sure enough, and some good intentions, but that's not at all what he needed. He could find that at a carnival or a Kiwanis meeting. Purpose and truth remained frustratingly elusive and vaguely defined. Of one thing he was certain: he didn't want his postmodern felt needs satisfied; he wanted them extinguished so he could get on with the real business of being who he was designed to be. What he'd just heard struck him as no more practical than ministering to an alcoholic by giving him a bigger bottle and then offering a more convenient place to vomit. He wanted rather to sober up and see the world for what it really was. That, he was beginning to realize, would mean looking farther back and higher up and somehow grasping the nature of a world he'd never seen and probably never could. Was that realism or escapism, he wondered? Maybe a realistic assessment of what it took to escape a life of shallow desires and uncontrolled appetites masquerading as needs, he decided. Either way, it didn't feel very uplifting. Oh well, he reasoned, a brand-new year was set to start in just a few hours and new starts bring unforeseen possibilities. Maybe everything would be crystal clear by this time tomorrow. A lot could happen between dusk and dawn, after all.

Elisha yawned, and only then did he realize how run-down he felt. The evening's raucous festivities had barely begun for most of his neighbors but for Elisha the night had already taken its toll, leaving him feeling as old and tired as the fading year. Late-night revelry didn't appeal to him, nor had it ever, really. He told himself he'd see in the New Year by watching the ball drop at Times Square, then call it a day.

The new neighbors, he saw, had other plans. Cars lined both sides of the street in front of the old Chancellor house and light poured forth from every window and chink on both floors. Already empty beer bottles filled a recycling bin that had been placed by the front door and partiers had taken to littering the front lawn with them. Elisha wondered what Mrs. Chancellor would think. For that matter, he wondered what Missy might be thinking. He guessed that the party was Compeyson's idea. It didn't seem like Missy's style.

He passed by the house half-expecting that he'd be spotted and invited inside, but no one paid him any attention, which suited him fine. He continued on to his own front door, let himself in, and then closed and locked it behind him. The glow from the brightly illuminated party next door bathed the living room in a sort of twilight and illuminated the path to the kitchen. Elisha followed it and retrieved his one and only New Year's Eve indulgence.

Opening a cupboard over the refrigerator, he fetched a half-full bottle of whiskey he had opened exactly one year ago, poured some into a glass, and topped it off with some cold ginger ale. With that, he returned to the living room, plopped himself down in his recliner, and turned on the television using the remote he kept tucked between the seat cushion and the armrest. Just a few seconds later, Miley Cyrus appeared, performing a hypnotic series of gyrations to the accompaniment of a song whose words he couldn't make out. Elisha watched without listening while he gulped his drink. By the time the crowd burst into applause, he noted to his own surprise that the glass was already empty and his head felt overly large and unnaturally far away. The emcee's voice replaced Miley's, but now Elisha was having difficulty understanding his words too, along with everyone else's. He set his glass down on the end table next to his chair, raised the footrest, and laid his head back against a pillow to relieve his tired neck of its weight.

On the screen, a commercial featuring a comically sad Great Dane wearing a conical party hat interrupted the celebrations at Times Square. It held Elisha's attention just long enough for him to note in a disinterested way that it was a pitch for a popular brand of cocktail peanuts. On cue, he began wishing he had some on hand. Moments later, the peanut commercial ended to make way for yet another ad. And then another, in a predictable and monotonous rhythm. The timer on the cable box indicated two hours before midnight, but Elisha knew he wouldn't make it that long. His eyes closed of their own accord, and he didn't resist. The flickering images projected from the television screen continued to bombard his closed eyelids and appeared to Elisha as dancing kaleidoscopic patterns of light and shadow that couldn't be shut out. The effects of the alcohol conspired with his fatigue and presently he felt himself falling. As he did, the amorphous patterns of light and darkness behind his eyelids morphed into recognizable images of people and things that had no business being in his living room.

A short while later—he had no idea how much time had passed—one of these shapes that had taken on the form of a tall man dressed like a carnival barker spoke, "Get up, Elisha. Step lively. I've got much to show you before dawn."

"Go away," Elisha responded impatiently. "I'm watching television."

"No, you're not. You've dozed off. It's after midnight. You've missed the start of the New Year."

"Big deal," Elisha grumbled, unimpressed. "I'll catch it on reruns. Now go away."

"Not until I've shown you the consequences of your actions. You are in danger, Elisha, and I'm here to guide you through the Slough of Despond."

"Watching television," Elisha mumbled once again, thinking that the words sounded familiar and wondering where he'd heard them before. "No time."

"'Would you so soon put out, with worldly hands, the light I give?' No, come. I've got a deal for you. One you won't want to miss. But it's only available for a limited time, so act now. Rise and walk with me!"

The words had a strange effect on Elisha, and without conscious effort, he found himself rising from his chair and floating slowly across the room in the direction of his unidentified visitor. The closer he approached, the more excitement he felt, and the more he wanted to continue in the same direction forever. But to his disappointment, he came to a stop alongside his companion and hovered, his feet not quite touching the floor. "I must be root beer," Elisha babbled, "because I'm afloat. But this is impossible. What's happening to me?"

"Bear but a touch of my hand *there*," said the visitor, laying it upon his heart, "and you shall be upheld in more than this!"

Again, the words sounded familiar to Elisha, but this time he remembered where he'd heard them. Or more precisely, where he had read them. "Oh drivel," he sputtered, "Am I in *that* story as well? Are you the Ghost of Christmas Past then?"

The visitor laughed. "Goodness no. He's a sentimental, idealistic, narrow-minded clod. I've no time for the likes of him. Nor should you. You can call me Virgil. I'm the Voice of Reason. And I've got something much more satisfying to show you than your past, and more real. Something that's too good to miss. In fact, you simply can't live without it. Happily, it can all be yours if you act now."

Elisha was intrigued and found himself wanting to hear more, but something in the tone of Virgil's voice shouted a warning into his soul, and he hesitated. "Does Christopher know you're here?" he asked, more insightfully than he knew.

"He does indeed," Virgil replied. "In fact, I'm here by his leave. He probably thinks it's for your own good, and it is to be sure, but not in the way he thinks. He does care for you, after all, bless him. But he's not very forthcoming. When the two of you had that little talk he didn't tell you everything you ought to know."

Elisha already knew that, or at least strongly suspected it. But it didn't seem like a good thing to admit to Virgil. Instead he asked, "You know about our conversation? How?"

"I was there all the time. You just didn't take notice of me. Christopher has that effect on people, curse him. Everything and everyone else seems to fade to insignificance in his presence. But I'm never really very far away from you, Elisha. And it's a good thing, or else you'd have made some irreversible mistakes by now. I'm here to make sure that doesn't happen."

"How?"

"By showing you the world as it really is, not as you seem to think it is. I've come to show you what's important and what's only imaginary. Like this so-called author you've been so concerned about in all those dreams you've been having of late."

"Like this one, you mean? But I can't remember any others. Not recently anyway. I usually remember my dreams. Do you?"

"Don't be absurd, Elisha. This isn't a dream. You're finally awake. I woke you. All those crazy ideas you've been having about an author and being in someone's story—those are the dreams. They aren't real. And it's about time you realized it, man."

"That's nuts," Elisha objected wearily. "Delicious cocktail nuts. Just look at me. I'm floating six inches above the ground, for crying out loud. How is that possible if this isn't a dream?"

Virgil laughed again, but this time in a not-so-friendly manner. "Don't be a simpleton. It's time for you to grow up. Just because you don't understand something is no reason to attribute it to a dream or to some manipulative unseen author. That's the way people used to think, sure enough. But we know better now. That age of myths and legends is over. I ended it. Those things are only suited for children these days, and dangerous enough at that. There are perfectly rational explanations for everything that happens."

"Like defying gravity?" Elisha chided.

"Gravity cannot be defied. It's an inflexible law of nature."

"That's easy for you to say," Elisha replied, unconvinced. "You've got both your feet on the ground. But what about me? I seem to have my head in the clouds, or very nearly."

"There you go again. I can see that I arrived not a moment too soon. Your case is serious."

"Now there we are in agreement," Elisha conceded. "Floating in midair is no laughing matter. It makes me uncomfortable, and I'm rather anxious about what might happen to me if the effect wears off without warning, when I'm halfway up a staircase, for instance. So if you have a rational explanation and you are really here to help me, then answer me. How and why am I floating about?"

"It's the multiverse," Virgil explained tolerantly and with complete conviction. Elisha said nothing but just raised both eyebrows to indicate that he found the explanation lacking in conviction. Virgil continued. "We live in a universe with set physical laws. As a result of those immutable laws, some things are possible and others aren't. They're against the rules, you see, and in this case, the rules can't be broken. All sorts of laws are theoretically possible, but only a few actually apply to our world. But in other universes completely different rules apply and things are possible that we would never dream of in our universe."

"But one of the rules of this here universe is that people don't float."

"No," Virgil went on. "You're wrong. That rule only applies in those dreams you've been having. Like I told you, you're awake now. This is a different universe than the one you're accustomed to. And in this world, people float. You see? It's perfectly rational and requires no speculative flights of fancy about things that can't be seen or proven."

"It doesn't?"

"Of course not. I've just explained how it doesn't. Pay attention Elisha or I won't be able to save you."

"From what?"

"From yourself first of all. And then from a life of dreary, colorless tedium. There's an exciting new world waiting for you outside your door, Elisha, a world you don't yet know."

"Do people float there?" Elisha quipped.

"As a matter of fact, they do," Virgil deadpanned. "And more than just that. Almost anything is possible out there. All you have to do is choose it, and it can be yours. Wouldn't you like to see what I can show you? I know you would. Don't deny it. That would be unnatural."

In spite of himself and an ethereal sensation of impending danger, Elisha felt a rush of excitement and a desire to comply. His life had indeed been a sheltered one. Undeniably so. He reflected regretfully on the many years he had passed without the slightest inkling that it was possible to float. What more had he missed out on by failing to explore beyond the boundaries of his boxed-in existence? And now here was a way to pull back the veil. Could he dare to walk away?

"Lead on," he heard himself say. His face, he realized, was set in a broad grin. For the briefest of moments, he wondered where it had come from and how it had gotten there, but then he attributed it to the multiverse, put it out of his mind, and followed Virgil outside, not bothering to open the front door, but simply passing through. But before he did, he cast a last look back over his shoulder and saw himself asleep in his recliner, still sitting in front of the television.

CHAPTER TWENTY THREE

Without Boundaries

*Do not move your neighbor's boundary stone set up by
your predecessors in the inheritance you receive in the
land the LORD your God is giving you to possess.*
—Deuteronomy 19:14

"Where are you taking me?" Elisha asked his guide.

"Not far," Virgil said reassuringly. "Something's about to happen that you need to see. Hurry now, I hadn't expected you to require so much convincing. We're running late. There's barely time." And with that, he increased his pace so that Elisha wouldn't have been able to keep up had he not been able to fly.

Seconds later, they arrived at an intersection not far from Elisha's house. The dimly lit streets seemed deserted in all directions. It struck Elisha as an unlikely destination if this was to be the scene of a momentous lesson, as Virgil implied. Elisha settled gracefully to the ground. In answer to the unspoken question implied by his puzzled glance, Virgil pointed to the center of the intersection and said, "Just watch. It won't be more than a few moments now."

Even as he spoke the words, Elisha noticed two distant head-lights. As they approached the intersection, they meandered unpredictably from one side of the street to the other and back in an irregular rhythm. "He's just come from a party," Virgil said, "where he drank enough for three men his size. He committed one or two other indiscretions as well, but those aren't important. It's the drinking that will provide the lesson you need to see. Oh, and you'll be wanting to take a few steps back. It won't be much of a lesson if you get killed in the process."

Elisha complied.

"Don't fail to notice that furry fellow over there as well," Virgil said, pointing to a short shadowy figure partially obscured by two garbage cans standing near a curb. It took Elisha a few seconds to identify it as a dog poking for scraps among the garbage. "Now just watch."

Elisha suspected he knew what he was being invited to witness and wondered whether he ought to intervene, but Virgil's caution against getting too close rooted his feet to the ground. Just as the swerving car approached the hound, and finding nothing to eat among the cans, the hungry dog seemingly decided to see if the scavenging was any better on the far side of the street. If so, it didn't matter. The car arrived before he finished crossing, struck him broadside, and made a sickeningly wet thud. The broken body briefly disappeared behind the passing vehicle, then reemerged, grotesquely flattened and motionless. The driver, oblivious to what he'd just done, continued on without pausing. "In the morning," Virgil foretold, "he'll arise late after sleeping off his hangover, walk outside to fetch his newspaper, and curse when he notices the crumpled grill and the dark hairs glued to his front end with dried blood. But he won't remember a thing, and he'll have no idea how it got there. He'll make an appointment to drop the car off at the body shop and in a few days the damage will be fixed. And that will be the end of it. No fuss, no grief, no memory. Nothing gained, nothing lost. Nothing of any significance, anyway."

"This was why you were in such a hurry, isn't it? You knew this was going to happen."

"We're here, aren't we? How else could I teach you this lesson? Make no mistake, Elisha. I didn't cause this accident. It was going to happen whether we were here to witness it or not. But if we hadn't been here, it would have been a wasted moment. This way, we can analyze it and interpret it and draw some useful conclusions."

"From the death of a hungry dog? What is there to learn?"

"That there is nothing to be learned from the death of a hungry dog. That it has no purpose. That assuming everything and everyone has a purpose is wrong and that trying to find meaning in anything and everything is a fool's errand. We're all here by mere chance. Nothing more. That dog was here because it was hungry. It could have gone in search of food in any of a hundred garbage cans up and down this street. But it picked these. Why? No reason. It just did. And that driver could have left his party at an infinite number of discrete moments in time, or not left at all. When he did leave, he could have taken any of several routes home. Of all those countless options, only one led inexorably to the death of that poor dog. Yet why did he choose the ones he did? No reason at all. He left when he did because that's when he felt like leaving. That's all. He took this way home because this is the street he always takes. Period. It's not destiny, or part of a plan, or a necessary plot twist or anything of the sort.

"Think, Elisha, and then put childish fantasies behind you. If an unseen author was writing this story, why would he have let this happen? Do you really suppose there's a profound cosmic purpose behind what happened here tonight? If so, I'd love to hear what it is. Go ahead, Elisha, do your best."

Elisha found himself at a loss for both words and answers. So Virgil offered some of his own. "Isn't it more reasonable to think that things just happen? That it's pointless to wonder why?"

Elisha didn't like the obvious answer to those questions, but he had no better ones to propose. He wondered idly whether it might be different if he hadn't had that drink while watching TV, or if that too had been meaningless. It seemed to him that the moonless night closed in around him, growing ever darker each time Virgil spoke.

"Take heart," his guide consoled him, "My purpose is not to bring you down, but to raise you up. I've shown you this accident to convince you that the path you've been walking these past few days leads only to pain, so you will be receptive to what I have to show you next. There are other ways, Elisha. Ways that you've neglected up till now but which will make you feel like you've been reborn if only you'll embrace them. Come with me and I'll show you."

"What choice do I have? I can't walk away now, not when I feel like this," Elisha replied miserably. "Lead on. I only hope that you're right."

"Fear not," Virgil hissed. "Fear is regressive. Put it behind you and look ahead to a world of new possibilities—a world where walking on air is the least of what you'll experience." With that, Virgil took Elisha's hand and the two of them ascended skyward, accelerating toward a bright point of light on the western horizon.

To Elisha, it resembled the morning twilight just before a brilliant sunrise and the start of a brand-new day, but it lay in the wrong direction. Ever faster they approached and steadily the light grew brighter. Soon it resolved itself into distinct patterns and ribbons that seemed to pulsate with life, much like veins and arteries carrying life-sustaining blood, only this blood seemed to glow with its own internal light. Then, in the twinkling of an eye, their forward motion ceased, and they hung suspended in space. Directly below them lay the source of the light, and for the first time, Elisha could make it out clearly. It was not blood vessels but roadways—a web of on ramps and cloverleafs, acceleration lanes and illuminated road signs, all bathed in the dazzling glare of countless streetlights. The pulsating motion that had given Elisha the impression of a living organism came from the head and taillights of endless lines of automobiles, entering and exiting the roadways and speeding off in all directions towards who-knew-where. The effect was dizzying and made Elisha's eyes hurt. He screwed them shut and turned away from the garish spectacle.

"No!" Virgil admonished him. "You mustn't do that. Take a closer look, Elisha. It's overwhelming at first, I'll grant, but in no time at all, you'll grow accustomed to it. In fact, you'll think it the most beautiful sight you've ever seen. Once you look at it and behold its beauty, you'll never be the same again."

Still Elisha hesitated.

"Go on, Elisha. Everyone looks eventually. You don't want to be left behind do you?"

Feeling extremely foolish, Elisha opened one eye just the tiniest bit, the way he used to do as a child when he went to the Saturday matinees and terrified himself by paying to watch a double feature of Hammer horror movies. Already, he noted, the glare did not seem quite as garish as it had.

"Imagine being in one of those cars down there," Virgil intoned. "You've never driven a car, have you, Elisha?"

Elisha honestly wasn't sure. He didn't think so. At least, he couldn't remember ever getting his license, or even a learner's permit. But until just a few days ago while talking with Mrs. Chancellor, he hadn't remembered learning to ride a bike. Virgil read his thoughts. "It's sad, isn't it? You've never known the joy of that freedom. Just look at those drivers. They enter the freeway wherever it pleases them and exit whenever they've reached their destination. If their first stop doesn't please them, they can get back on any time they like, and head off again in whatever direction suits their fancy. You've never known the rush of unrestrained freedom. But you can. Look closer,

Elisha. Read some of the road signs and see where each off ramp leads. Then imagine yourself heading toward each destination."

Curiosity got the better of Elisha's fear, and he looked with both eyes. "Career," read the first. "Success," said the next. Just this side of an especially convoluted tangle of intertwined over and under-passes stood a series of arrows indicating the way to "Ego," "Status," "Money," and "Prestige." Yet another unusually large sign loomed over a particularly congested stretch of highway: "Yield to No One." Beyond, past a series of forks that much of the traffic seemed determined to reach, a series of exits bore the labels "Expedience," "Relativism," and "Personal Choice."

"Isn't it intoxicating?" Virgil cooed. "And you don't have to choose just one exit. You can go round and round as much as you like, sampling the pleasures of each, and no one will ever tell you to stop or to go in another direction. If they dare, we'll quickly weed them out. All you need to do is get onto the highway and start driv-ing. There's a road to every possible destination, and as long as you accept my invitation, they are all open to you. But wait, see the con-sequences of intolerance." As he watched, streetlights began to go out and one by one new signs replaced those Elisha had already seen, each reading "Road Closed," or "Do Not Enter."

"That's the choice Christopher is offering you—a stultifying world of rules and boundaries and narrow-minded prohibitions. But that's regressive. The world has tried that and just look at where it's all led. Oh, it served a purpose for a time, of course, but those old ways have long since outlived their usefulness. Their time is over. Those old rules are senile, like those who obey them. But if you just agree to cast them off you can set your own course, without limits. You can start all over, like a child, a young and vibrant youth with his whole life ahead of him. So cast off restraint. Once you do, there's no telling where you can go. No telling at all. But you'll never see until you are reborn."

"How can a man be reborn when he is old?" Elisha heard someone say before realizing that the voice was his own. "Surely he cannot enter a second time into his mother's womb!"

"How can it be that you have not heard all these things before now?" Virgil chided. "The spirit of the times is changing. It's brimming with endless possibilities, but only for those bold enough to claim it. You can be among them, Elisha. You deserve to be among them. Don't be regressive. Come with me. Together we'll explore each and every byway of this brave new world where you'll never bump up against a single boundary, and no one will ever tell you what you can and can't do. All you need to do is tell me yes."

Elisha felt very much as if he wanted to agree and certainly would have were it not for a faint knocking sensation that grew in his subconscious. He felt sure it was a sound, yet at first he felt it rather than heard it, pushing back against his inclination to listen more attentively to Virgil's offer. With each repeated *thump, thump, thump*, it grew in intensity and urgency. As it built to a crescendo, all other sensations seemed to flee before it, and as they did, Elisha's head grew clearer and things that had seemed so beautiful just moments before took on frightening form. Other things that had seemed true now took on the unmistakable shape of lies, and Elisha wondered how he had managed to confuse the two. And still the pounding persisted, ever louder and at an increasing tempo. They were clearly audible sounds now, but in their intensity, they still struck against Elisha almost like blows from an invisible fist.

Elisha was surprised to hear Virgil still talking in a normal conversational tone, now barely discernable above the increasing din. In fact, he seemed completely unaware of it. Elisha could just barely make out his words. "No boundaries," he was still saying. "No rules. Here you are free do whatever you choose—there's nothing to prevent you from doing anything you want to do, or claiming whatever you see for your own."

At once, Elisha knew what he most wanted to do. He reeled back and, putting everything he had into the blow, struck Virgil across the jaw with his balled fist, something he had never done in the regressive world of boundaries. "So sorry, chap, but I really, really wanted to do that," he told the unconscious form lying crumpled at his feet. "I was sure you'd approve." He bent over, reached into Virgil's pants pocket, removed his wallet, and emptied it of its cash. "And I claim this for my own," he added, stuffing the bills into his own pocket. Then, turning his back on the brightly lit darkness, he put one foot in front of the other and began walking back home, not in defiance of the law of gravity, but in cooperation with it.

Behind him, an ambulance approached Virgil's motionless form. Graham Ripper climbed out and shook his head at the sight of Virgil lying in the gutter. He lifted the body onto his shoulders, heaved it through the rear doors of his emergency vehicle, then climbed back behind the wheel. In a matter of seconds, the ambulance had floated away.

The pounding didn't cease. It grew still louder and clearer and soon Elisha could think of nothing else. It seemed ready and able to sweep him away or else swallow him whole. He shook his head in frantic desperation and screwed his eyelids shut, as if that might somehow keep out the sound. When he opened them again, he was in his own living room, in his own chair, in front of the television set, which was running an old black-and-white movie. The clock indicated that it was 4:13 a.m. The thumping remained, but now he had no trouble identifying it as the sound of someone knocking on his front door. But not just knocking; it sounded as though someone was prepared to pound it to pieces in order to get inside.

Elisha jumped from his chair, in an instant wide awake, turning this way and that, trying to distinguish what sort of emergency he had nearly slept through, and fearing that the house was on fire. He could see nothing amiss. He opened the door and nearly took a rap in the face from Missy, his neighbor.

"Elisha! Are you all right?" she gasped, reaching out to touch his face. "Oh, thank heavens you are! I was so afraid I'd be too late!" And with that, she burst into tears and embraced him.

CHAPTER TWENTY FOUR

Faerie Tales

"Who shut up the sea behind doors
when it burst forth from the womb,
when I made the clouds its garment
and wrapped it in thick darkness,
when I fixed limits for it
and set its doors and bars in place,
when I said, 'This far you may come and no farther;
here is where your proud waves halt'?
—Job 38:8–11

Elisha self-consciously hugged Her in return, feeling somehow that he owed it to her but also that it wasn't entirely right. He wondered whether Compeyson knew she was here, or if he might once against step unexpectedly through the door and catch them being rather too familiar. In spite of himself, Elisha began chuckling. He was back in a world of rules and old-fashioned morality, and he liked it. He released Missy and stepped away, only then noticing that she wore a nightgown and robe, with slippers on her feet.

She wiped tears from her face with the back of her hands, but remained visibly upset. "Would you mind getting me a drink?

Something cold, I mean. Not a drink, that is, just something to drink." Elisha smiled but understood. He helped her into the kitchen.

He opened the orange juice for the first time once again, knowing that Christopher would approve, and poured Missy a glassful. "I'm sorry I can't offer you any cookies. I don't bake. Would you like some store-bought soda crackers?"

"No. no. This is fine, thank you." She gulped down a mouthful of the juice, then took a deep breath followed by a long, slow exhale and a shudder, as if releasing still-pent-up anxiety.

"So exactly what sort of trouble did you think I was in, and why?" Elisha asked once she had composed herself. Missy waved her hand dismissively, as if embarrassed over wasting her neighbor's time with her misguided mission of mercy. "No, tell me," Elisha persisted. "It's important that you tell me."

"So you'll know what to say when they come to take me away?" Missy wondered out loud. "Oh, Elisha, I'm so sorry for scaring you. You must think I'm daft."

"Why would I think that?"

"Why wouldn't you? Do you normally have neighbors show up in a panic at all hours and wake you from a sound sleep?"

"It wasn't all that sound."

Missy assumed it was an attempt at humor. "Whatever," she said, with yet another dismissive wave.

"No, really," Elisha insisted. "You weren't mistaken. I *was* in danger. Your knocking came not a moment too soon. I might have ruined everything if you hadn't woken me. How did you know?"

Tears dripped from Missy's sightless eyes. She still suspected Elisha might be teasing her or at least spinning a yarn intended to alleviate her embarrassment. But Elisha repeated the question in a tender, sincere tone that left her with no doubt that he was in earnest and genuinely grateful.

"What happened here tonight?" she asked, ignoring Elisha's own twice-asked question.

Elisha decided he owed her the privilege. "To be honest, I'm not really sure. It may have been just a dream, but I fear not. Even so, you rescued me from quite a frightening nightmare, at the very least. More likely, it was something far worse. It feels even now like my very soul hung in the balance—like some sort of spell had me in its grip and tested my resolve. I fear I would have crumbled and struck a deal with the devil if you hadn't called me back home."

"Is that what I did?" Missy gasped. Her voice sounded brittle, and Elisha could tell she didn't fully comprehend but accepted his assurance without question nonetheless. He sensed that a lifetime of walking by faith rather than sight had made her quite good at trusting in things that couldn't be seen.

"It is," Elisha affirmed. "And you have my thanks. My fate hung in the balance. I was both dead and alive and yet neither, until you came looking for me and death gave way to life. Just like with Schrödinger's cat. It seems your mother named you well. But now, it's your turn. Tell me what made you come over and knock for me."

Missy turned her eyes in Elisha's direction, just as a sighted person might if trying to read the expression on his face. "Honestly, I don't know. I just felt a nudge, that's all. Well, more than a nudge, really, an overpowering compulsion. I was lying in bed. I think I was asleep, but I'm not sure. We had a party earlier this evening—last evening, that is—to celebrate the new year."

"Yes, I know," Elisha said. "I noticed as I walked home last night. It surprised me that you'd found so many people to invite, being new to the neighborhood and all."

Missy gave another of her waves of the hand, and Elisha assumed she must frequently employ the gesture to take the place of troublesome explanations. She clearly didn't like talking unless she had something significant to say.

"Oh that was Compeyson. He invited his new bank coworkers over without asking me. They're a lively bunch. He hit it off with them right away, but I just didn't fit in, so I spent the whole evening in the bedroom and was exhausted by the time things broke up. But then something came over me. Something like women's intuition, but not entirely. I've had a sense about things before and... well, you know all about that, don't you? But this went well beyond just some vague notion or odd feeling in my gut. The closest thing I've ever felt to it was that feeling I had before moving here—the one we told you about. The one that convinced us to move even though we could think of no clear reason why we should. But even that pales in comparison to what I felt tonight. That previous feeling grew steadily over the course of several days and weeks until it gradually overpowered my doubts and fears. Tonight, I felt an instantaneous urgency that left no room for doubt whatsoever."

She tugged at the hem of her robe. "I don't even remember putting this on. I don't know what I thought I'd find or even why I headed here. I acted purely on instinct. I found myself banging on your front door, completely heedless of the cold, before I realized what I was doing. You didn't answer right away and I couldn't help myself. I just kept knocking harder and faster. Just look, I banged my knuckles raw." She stopped to take another deep breath. "I know that doesn't really answer your question, Elisha, but it's the best way I can describe it."

"And Compeyson?"

"As far as I know, he's still sound asleep in bed. He did a good bit of drinking earlier and was dead to the world. Whatever happened to me didn't affect him, and I didn't bother pausing to rouse him. There wasn't time. Or it didn't seem like there was anyway, but even now I don't know what made me think so."

"You'd probably best be getting back home. If he wakes up, it'll be his turn to think you've run out on him." Elisha felt confident he could get away with a little humor without offending her and hoped it might do her some good to have cause to smile. He was right. She grinned wearily and nodded. "But I want to reassure you once more," Elisha added. "Don't question your intuition. Your premonitions seem to have a way of proving trustworthy. You did the right thing. You needn't try to explain it. Things happen for a reason. I believe that. And everything turned out for the best."

"What should I tell Compeyson?"

"Tell him whatever you think best or nothing at all, if you prefer. If you're the only one who felt this compulsion, then it was meant just for you. He doesn't need to understand. Since everything turned out well, he probably won't even be very interested. He'll likely just be glad you didn't wake him."

"But what if this happens again?"

"I can't make any guarantees, but I'm fairly certain it won't. Your premonition clearly had something to do with my, well, my dream or vision or whatever it was, and that ended pretty decisively, thanks to you. I don't suppose I'll have another, so unless I'm mistaken your job is done." Elisha thought it best to leave it at that and not get into what tended to happen to acquaintances of his who achieved their purpose.

"One more thing though before you go. The other night, I asked your husband about his interests and vocation, but I never got around to asking you the same thing. I'm curious. Have you always been a housewife?"

"Oh no. Before I met Compeyson, I was a librarian."

"Really?" Elisha chuckled. "Tell me, how did a librarian win the heart of someone who doesn't like to read? I'll bet it's a good story."

"Not really. We hired him to audit the library's books, and I took him down to the basement to show him where we kept the records and then, well…" She blushed and said no more.

"So you love books?" Elisha asked to fill the silence.

"I love stories," she corrected him. "My mom used to read me stories all the time. She said she wasn't going to allow my blindness to be an excuse for missing out on the classics. I loved the hours and hours we spent together with her books. For as long as I can remember, I've liked to imagine myself as one of the characters in those stories she shared with me." She hid her face in her hands. "I guess that makes me sound pretty childish."

"On the contrary," Elisha assured her, "it makes you a prophet. You see things other people don't. It's a rare gift. Treasure it."

He guided her back through the living room and toward the door as they spoke. Pausing long enough to wrap his own overcoat around her before sending her back home, Elisha opened the door for Missy, and she stood on the threshold, on the verge of stepping through. There, framed by the doorway, she paused, then turned to face Elisha. In her sightless eyes, he saw both transcendent joy and immanent sadness.

"I feel like I'm part of a story that's coming to an end. I believe— no, I'm certain—that once I pass through this door I won't see you again, Elisha. Ever. I don't understand why, because we're neighbors, but I just know this is our final goodbye. I wish it were otherwise."

"Have no regrets," he begged her. "I understand now. This was why you moved here. For this very evening. It was your purpose—to be here at the critical moment when I most needed a friend. Before you arrived, I didn't have one. That was your purpose, and you played your part to perfection." Elisha wasn't sure, but it seemed to him that Missy was crying again. "And we will see each other again. Every time anyone reads our story, we'll meet outside my door, and you'll invite me into your kitchen and offer me some of your cookies, and you'll come to my rescue dressed in a robe and slippers—a beautiful damsel rushing to the rescue of a knight in distress."

The thought seemed to please her. "You've explained my purpose, Elisha. But how about you? What will you do next?"

"I don't know. I feel like I've been wandering aimlessly in a fog, unable to find my destination. My own purpose is more than I've been able to see."

"I think maybe I can help you with that, Elisha. All your life you've loved books. You've read them voraciously. You've been a gatherer collecting ideas passed down through the ages and given voice by the characters in your books. You've even started writing one or two yourself, haven't you?"

Elisha shook his head in utter amazement, then caught himself, and whispered, "Yes."

"You shouldn't have given up so easily. That is your purpose. You weren't created to enjoy stories, like me, but to write your own. You are meant to become a creator in your own right, or a subcreator at least, and breathe new worlds into existence, to inhabit them with characters who can look farther back and higher up than we can, and find hope in what they see. That's your purpose, Elisha, and it's high time you get started."

"How do you know all this?" Elisha gasped.

Missy smiled. "I see it. And my premonitions have a way of proving trustworthy." A playful smile graced her sad face. "Now it's time to go. I really don't quite understand what happened to you this evening, Elisha, but I'm very glad that I was able to help you. Happy New Year. Make it a good one. Give it some purpose. Write a good story. Now goodbye." She turned again and walked through the doorway, vanishing into the darkness beyond the porch light.

Elisha retraced his steps back across his living room and into his easy chair, stopping first to turn off the television, which had been on the entire evening. For quite a while, he sat alone in the darkness and the silence. He enjoyed their company. They seemed well behaved after the garish lights and noise of his vision. On impulse, he reached into his pocket and pulled out a crumpled wad of money.

Dawn would arrive soon, and he thought it pointless to go back to sleep. Sleep would not have come to him at any rate, he knew. Instead, he sat thinking about everything Missy had said— not just this evening, but from the moment he first saw her in Mrs. Chancellor's front yard. He smiled.

Then, reaching toward the end table that stood next to his chair, and opening the drawer, he rummaged through its contents until he found the pencil and stenographer's notebook he almost remembered putting there. In the pale light of the rising sun, he began to write. Where to begin? With so much he needed to say, how could he begin? As soon as he posed the question the most natural place—the only possible place—became crystal clear to him, and in a great rush, words began pouring forth: "In the beginning…"

It Is Finished....

Dear Reader,

The story that flowed from Elisha's hand was wondrously wrought, but it is not meant for your world. It is for his world only, and you are not privileged to read it. Your Author created you for this world, and it is in this world that you must find your inspiration, your hope, and your creative purpose. It's time you get started. Your life is a story. Start writing it. New worlds wait for you to imagine into existence. Stories tinged with sadness wait to be written and told. Stories brimming with laughter and joy need to be penned. Some stories bring new life to the dying, and others convict the self-satisfied soul of sloth. What kind of story will you write? We shall see. I will be watching with great expectations.

It is finished.

—*Christopher*

About the Author

Bruce Warren Heydt has spent twenty-three years in the trade and consumer magazine publishing business, employed first by The Chilton Company in Radnor, Pennsylvania, and then by Primedia Special Interest Publications in Harrisburg, Pennsylvania. For most of this time, he served as managing editor of British Heritage magazine.

His freelance feature articles have appeared in such publications as *Historic Traveler, American History Illustrated, Christian History and Biography, The Annals of Eastern Pennsylvania*, published by the Eastern Pennsylvania Conference of the United Methodist Church, and *Reader's Digest Books*.

More recently, Bruce has filled the role of teaching pastor at Millersville Community Church in Lancaster County, Pennsylvania.

He currently lives with his wife, Susan, in Mount Joy, Pennsylvania. Bruce is the father of three children—sons Scott and Ben and daughter Kristin, who helped inspire this book. His passions include reading, writing, searching for his Author, and pursuing his purpose. *Things Unseen* is Bruce's first novel.

CPSIA information can be obtained
at www.ICGtesting.com
Printed in the USA
LVHW01s2010170118
563092LV00001B/105/P